Little 15

Little 15

Stephanie Saye

Bad Doggy Productions
Dallas, Texas

Second Edition
Copyright © Stephanie Saye, 2013
All rights reserved.

Bad Doggy Productions
Dallas, Texas

Edited by Christina M. Frey
Cover art by JR Rapier
Cover Design by Brent Meske
Author Photograph by Jamie Armijo Photography

ISBN: 978-0-9897483-3-9

Printed in the United States of America

To the Laurens of the world. May you find peace and healing.

This then is my story. I have reread it. It has bits of marrow sticking to it, and blood, and beautiful bright-green flies. At this or that twist of it I feel my slippery self eluding me, gliding into deeper and darker waters than I care to probe.

—Vladimir Nabokov, *Lolita*

Chapter 1

It was only a matter of time before I called him.

I'd gone around and around with my therapist on this, how unhealthy it was keeping any sort of connection, knowing that he'd never change. "We call people like your father 'unmovable,'" Celia would tell me. "But you, well, you've moved."

And moved I had during the last ten years of sitting on Celia's blue and green plaid sofa for one hour each week, for one glorious and sometimes painful hour of ripping the scabs off my emotional pain. Yet sometimes I wondered if I'd really moved all that much.

"Most people can't make the changes that you have—it just gets too painful," she would say on days I felt weak. "So they eventually give up and go back to their dysfunctional ways, out of nothing more than a need to relieve their own guilt. They step back into the cycle of allowing the same people to hurt them, to control them, and then they lose themselves all over again. This time harder, and more severe."

Maybe that's what I was doing that morning as I picked up the phone and dialed my dad's number, the man whom I hadn't spoken to in more than a year. I knew I was breaking the rules. Celia had made me promise that I'd call her whenever I felt the overwhelming urge to surrender to the hot pain of my guilt.

But that day I ignored all of it, all the therapy work I'd done to reconstruct what guilt and shame had destroyed. I ignored the child Lauren pleading inside me. I ignored the adult Lauren, the forty-year-old Lauren, the mature woman who finally understood what was best for her. I ignored it all, except for the guilt. Oh no, the guilt that day was unforgiving.

"Hello."

He answered. This time he actually answered, but there was no life in his voice. He spoke from a hollow shell.

"Dad?"

"Yeah."

"It's Lauren."

"Yeah."

"How are you?"

"Well, I'm still here, aren't I?" He sounded disappointed. After all these years, God still hadn't answered his prayer for death.

"And that's a good thing, right?"

"If that's how you want to look at it."

I could hear the TV on in the background. Crowds cheering. A whistle blowing. "Whatcha watching?"

"Um, North Carolina and Duke."

"Do you think North Carolina has a chance of knocking them out this year?"

"Sure. I mean, if they want it. They've got to want it."

How quickly our conversation had found its way over to basketball. Always basketball. But I knew better than to take the trap.

"I'm seeing someone."

"Uh huh."

"He's a really nice person."

"You don't say."

"It's going well, Dad." I was determined to stay positive.

"Let me guess, fifteen to twenty years older?"

"That's not fair!" I said. "He's the same age as me."

"Really. Still, why bother?"

"What do you mean?"

"Well, it won't make a difference anyway . . . . at least it didn't to your mother."

"Dad—"

"Nowadays when things get rough, people just leave. There's no sanctity in marriage anymore."

"You gave Mom no choice. You didn't want to change."

"Let marriage be held in honor among all, and let the marriage bed be undefiled, for God will judge the sexually immoral and adulterous."

"Dad, you know that's not what happened."

"She's married to someone else, isn't she? Were we not married in the Catholic Church? Is our marriage not still considered sacred and bound?"

"Dad!"

"And is she not committing adultery right at this moment?"

"This is your warning, Dad." I didn't recognize my own voice. "I've told you before I'm not gonna discuss this."

"What the hell do you know about marriage? Except how to destroy them!"

The guilt that had been right on my heels leaped up and latched onto my back. I'd always been easy prey.

"You can't talk to me like that anymore."

"Is that what your shrink tells you to say? But does your shrink know how much I've done for you? How much I've sacrificed? Does the fifth commandment mean anything to you?"

My flight side kicked in and I ended the call, then tossed the phone to the other end of the sofa as if it had burned me. Though my skin felt no pain, my head and my chest were searing with it. My father was that poisonous to me, even after twenty-five years.

Perhaps he was right. How much of it really was my fault? His marriage, Daniel's marriage, and my own life in between. Looking back, it's all kind of a muddle. It's foggy and shady and mixed up, even on my better days. I know it was wrong, and even though I've said a million times in therapy that it wasn't my fault, that I was just a kid, it's not so clear to me. Especially when I wake up in a cold sweat with that scene playing over and over again in my head.

Always the same scene. I see a basketball court, and a younger me, and Daniel, my coach. I'm running suicide drills.

He's blowing his whistle or clapping his hands, yelling, "Faster," and I pick up speed. He smiles and I get so lost in it that I slam into the wall. Hard. But the wall isn't a wall; it's a row of lockers, and I see my locker from back in high school. There's something written on it in black marker, a Sharpie. But I can't make it out, so I squint until the letters come into focus.

WHORE.

It's written in big capital letters. I fall back a couple steps and then feel Daniel come up behind me. He runs his hand down my back, right to the small of it, then stops and moves it further down. I am pulsing and warm. And then I wake up and I can smell him. I can hear him. I can almost feel him.

My eyes open and I look over at the man in my bed, but my mind always replays the reel of another. I move through the scenes of how it all happened, every detail of that so-called happier time, when he was all I knew, all I hoped for and all I dreamed of. If only I could escape there again, just for a while, twenty-five years into the past.

Chapter 2

If I could escape there, this is what I would see, that Saturday morning in the spring of '89, near the end of my freshman year of high school. I was instructing my first piano student, a seven-year-old boy named Ethan Clarke. I was not what you would call a musical prodigy, but I'd been playing the piano since I was five. Ten years later, I was playing it for money. Well, getting paid to help other people play it, or at least that was the plan. Money was tight in our house, so my sister and I had to earn it. She worked in a French bakery after school, and I taught the piano to young Ethan, who, I distinctly recall, resented every damn minute of it.

On that morning, as I sat there resisting the urge to wring Ethan's neck, a cacophony of voices rang out from the entryway. They sounded foreign to me, unsettling and dangerous. One was that of a man, deep and powerful like a bullhorn; the other like a squawking bird, pitchy and irritating. I swallowed several times to calm myself, to quell the lump rising in my throat, but it didn't help me feel better. Deep down, I knew the visitors had come for me.

I wanted to leave the room, walk out the front door and lose myself in the lazy neighborhood of oak trees and ranch-style homes. Instead I stayed put, trying to focus on Ethan banging away at "Three Blind Mice" on my parents' upright Yamaha. I wound the metronome and set it to the appropriate speed to help steady Ethan's rhythm. Its tick-tick-tocking only added to my anxiety, punctuating every missed note and sorry excuse for a melody. I leaned over and placed my hands over Ethan's. "Stroke, don't hit," I told him. "Relax your fingers and touch the keys loosely, like this." I lightly shook his small hands to relax them, rounding his knuckles and gently pressing his fingers on the keys.

My own hands were thick and clammy, a pair of "Division I basketball hands," my dad would always say. Nothing I did could make them look any less manly. Even my silver dangle rings seemed to accentuate their size.

My attention snapped back as Ethan started to fidget under my palms. I let go of his hands and instructed him to start again from the top, this time taking care to keep his fingers rounded. The metronome clicked on. Ethan glared at me with pursed lips, perhaps hoping to intimidate me into ending the lesson early. He held this stare for a good while and then, bored with the game, turned back to the sheet music in front of him. He began to pound harder than ever, flattening his fingers to exaggerate the thumping sound on the keys. I didn't make any attempt to correct him. I just sat there watching, letting him bang away on the ivories. I let him—as I did every Saturday morning— make a mockery of me.

The partition doors swung open, and my mom poked her head in.

"How much longer 'til the lesson's over?" she said to me.

"Why?"

"Lauren," she said, sounding almost desperate. "Your father invited some people here to see you."

"Can I go now, Ms. Lauren?" Ethan's eyes brightened at the possibility of the lesson ending early. Why his mother forced him to take piano lessons was beyond me; it was obvious that the boy hated them. Before I could answer Ethan's question, my mother told him he could go watch cartoons until his mom arrived. He bolted from the room as I turned sharply to address my mother.

"Who are they?"

"Lauren, just come to the kitchen," she urged. "Please . . . don't make your father wait."

"Mom, no!" I pounded my fist on the piano bench. "Tell me who they are!"

My mom sighed and folded her arms. "Coach Krum and Sister Louvois from Saint Agnes."

I made it very clear to my mother that I wasn't interested in talking to anyone from Saint Agnes, a school for snobby rich kids smack-dab in the middle of one of the most affluent areas of Dallas. I was in such a huff that I jabbed my bony hip on the edge of the piano as I stomped out of the room. Rubbing away the pain, I ran down our dark hall toward my room, my long, lanky legs covering two strides at once. I shut the door and sat hard on my bed, sinking into the springs. The stuffed animals piled on my floral comforter toppled to the floor, but I didn't want to expend the energy to lean down and pick them up off the shag carpet. They no longer held the same importance they had when I was a child, and seeing no need for them now that I was a teenager, I shoved them under the bed with my heels. I guess I was hoping they'd just go away, just like those stupid people from St. Agnes.

I remember the air feeling musty and damp; Dad was always stingy about turning on the air conditioner. I walked over and pulled back the orange curtain that for years had been baked by the sun. Rays of sunshine beamed into my room, dulled slightly by the mucky film of dust on the window. I ran my finger along the windowpane in a downward motion, leaving a clear line behind.

It's not that I was a brat or a difficult fifteen-year-old; I just wanted my life to remain simple and uncomplicated. I wanted to play the piano and be left alone. But my father had envisioned another path for me, one that didn't involve a single melody. The people he had invited to our house that day were part of his grand plan to make me a star—a plan he reminded me of over and over, any chance he got.

"I never had anyone to encourage me like you have," he would tell me when he was feeling particularly low. "You should be thankful."

"I am, Dad, I am thankful," I would say, trying my best to sound convincing.

"It's God's will that makes you this way . . . gives you such talent."

"Yes. God. It's His will," I'd repeat. I wanted to be sure that my dad knew I was listening.

"God didn't think I deserved it when I was your age, so He gave it to you. And now we must treasure it and use it wisely, as if we were going to die tomorrow. Let's bow our heads and ask God for wisdom."

And then we would pray. No matter where we were or what we were doing, my father would expect me to bow my head in prayer. It didn't matter how many people stared. "Let them," my father would say. "For they are of the weak-minded."

But on that Saturday morning, I was the one feeling weak-minded and intimidated when my father came and stood before me in my room, ordering me to look him in the eye as he explained to me why I would be switching schools. Yes, that's why I was so upset. To a high school freshman, switching schools was the end of the world.

"Coach Krum has seen you play, Lauren, and he wants you on his team," my father said in his deep, throaty drawl. We sat there on my bed, sinking into the mattress. The sides of our thighs touched, so I rose slightly and moved over, for there was something strangely awkward in having physical contact with my father. I distinctly remember folding my arms over my chest to downplay the size of my breasts; I didn't want him to know that I had grown into a woman, to draw attention to what puberty had done.

My father must have sensed my uneasiness that day, because he cleared the phlegm from his throat with an abrupt and forceful cough. He began speaking, as he always did, of God, our Heavenly Father. "We've talked about this before. God has blessed you with tremendous talent . . . talent I never had but wanted so badly," he said. "You must know this."

I did know. I knew exactly what he was talking about. I knew that I could easily score twenty points in a single basketball game. I knew I could take on two defenders at once, juke them and come away clean with barely an increase in my breathing.

From the day my father had first handed me a basketball, I had known exactly what to do with it. But what I didn't know how to do was break the news to my father that I wasn't as in love with the game as he was. I mean, I liked the game well enough. There was a certain power that came with pushing up off the ground and suspending in midair, the ball rolling off the tips of my fingers into the net with a swoosh. Yet basketball wasn't my life, wasn't my reason for being.

But for my father, it was everything. I was his second chance at a career that had eluded him. I held the talent, the natural ability that at my age he had only dreamed of having.

He began again, this time in a more authoritative tone. "Lauren, you'll be starting at Saint Agnes in the fall. Now it's time for you to come meet your new coach."

Looking back—and I'm sure you'd agree—it was a good deal. All I had to do was play basketball and maintain a B minus average, and in return I would get to attend the most prestigious Catholic all-girls school in the city. I should have been grateful for the opportunity. I should have considered myself lucky that the leaders of this elite institution were giving me, an ordinary teenage girl of humble upbringing, a shot at greatness. Instead I wanted to close my eyes and make it all go away. The truth was that I just didn't want to start over again at a brand new school, even if Saint Agnes did have the best girls' basketball team around.

My father gave a long sigh and stood up. He knew he was at odds with me but didn't quite know how to proceed. And that's when we heard a rap on my bedroom door.

"Come in," said my father.

The door opened slowly without disturbing the jingle bells dangling from the door hook. Then the blood drained from my face.

"I hope I'm not interrupting. Mrs. Muchmore said it was okay to poke my head in."

It was Coach Krum. Coach Daniel Krum, that is. The famed and very beloved Coach Krum who had led the Lady Lambs to two consecutive district titles in just five years. The same man who was credited by the local sports media for helping put the all-girls Catholic high school on the map in a city where mostly public schools ruled the leader board. The same Daniel Krum who had managed to do all that before the age of thirty-five.

"No, not at all, Daniel," said my father. "Please come in and join us."

There was a moment of awkward silence as Daniel Krum looked around for a place to sit. I was mortified. There in my room was the head basketball coach for Saint Agnes, and in plain view, only a few inches from his feet, rested a wadded pair of my underwear. All I wanted to do was curl up and die. I watched in silent panic as Coach Krum moved the wicker chair from my desk—the chair with the dirty clothes hanging over the backside—to the middle of the room. He mounted it like a motorcycle and leaned his weight forward on the chair's legs. Trying to avoid his gaze and nervously chewing my bottom lip, I glanced up long enough to see that he had on khaki pants and a white Saint Agnes oxford shirt.

"Lauren, I'm Coach Krum."

Feeling uneasy and still soured by my parents' decision, I paused before I shook the hand that he so abruptly had shoved in my direction. When I finally placed my hand in his, he held it firmly, confirming without mistake the reason for his visit. "Let me get right to the point," he said. His eyes were small but memorable, and piercingly blue.

"Four years ago, I started to build my team. I had nothing but freshmen, a few sophomores and a couple of juniors and seniors. By the time those freshmen were juniors, we had won state. Now those same freshmen are graduating, and I need to find the next generation to keep our winning streak."

As he spoke, his thick, reddish-brown mustache drew my gaze to his lips, and then to the second-day stubble covering his jaw and cheekbones.

"Every year we do a bit of scouting, and your name keeps coming up." Coach Krum pointed at me, waving his index finger. "I've watched you and I like what I see. Never mind the Saint Agnes game." He paused for a moment. "Your nerves got the best of you that night, and with some solid coaching, I can help you overcome that. I can make you better."

Ah, the Saint Agnes game. After that night, I had vowed to never play basketball again. It was one of the last games of the season and probably the most important. There was about a minute and a half left to play, and I had the ball about midcourt, looking for an open man. The Saint Agnes girls were all over us. Then out of nowhere, the Saint Agnes crowd—we were on their home turf—started counting down: "Five . . . four . . . three . . . two . . . one . . ." I panicked. Under the impression that we were down to seconds, I heaved the ball from half court as hard as I could. It was a perfect air ball and ended up in the hands of a Saint Agnes forward, who quickly ran it down court for two points. I stood there stunned, unaware that there was still more than a minute left in the game. The crowd had tricked me. The gym roared with laughter and I was quickly benched.

The memories of that night, and the embarrassment, came rushing back like a wound being torn open. I sat there on my mushy mattress, staring down at my sneakers and the stuffed animals on the floor.

I think that at that point, Daniel Krum thought he had lost me. If he had known me a little better, he would have realized that my silence was my way of submitting to his request—or rather, to my father's request. My father was making this all look very democratic, but in the end it didn't matter what I wanted. It never had in the first place.

Leaning lower on the edge of the chair, Daniel Krum balanced on the balls of his feet and rocked back and forth. "I wouldn't blame you if you didn't want to come play for Saint Agnes. That game was a hard lesson. But the crowds you'll face down the road in college will be twice as ruthless—especially if you get recruited by any of the Big Twelve teams. And you will, I guarantee it, if you come play for me."

Chapter 3

Daniel Krum had long since left when I finally decided to emerge from my room. I had fretted away most of the afternoon, wondering how I'd break the news to my best friend, June, that she'd have to start her sophomore year without me. I didn't know how to tell her that I no longer could sit next to her at our favorite lunch table and that I wouldn't be around for her to pass notes to between classes or to complain to about the bitches in the snotty crowd.

June and I didn't know what it was like to be apart; we'd been joined at the hip since first grade. I really didn't have any other friends besides her, or at least no one else I could call a best friend. And now that I think about it, she didn't either up until that time. This was almost more frightening than the thought of telling June I was transferring to Saint Agnes. But she was smart and pretty, and wouldn't have a problem finding a crowd to hang out with. And really, she wouldn't have to find them; they'd find her. That would leave me in my crisp new Saint Agnes uniform to explore the open waters on my own, with no one to toss me a life raft when my head sunk below the water line.

I think June ended up calling a couple times that afternoon, along with the usual handful of callers for my sister. But that afternoon I purposely let the answering machine pick up the phone, not knowing the right words to say if it was her.

Through the thin wall separating my sister's room from mine, I kept hearing the machine click on, greeting callers to an obnoxious recording of some punk rock song. Then my sister's sultry voice would come on the line: "Hey, it's Carla. You know the drill." I listened to that over and over and even caught myself sarcastically mouthing the words along with the machine. I was trying to sleep, but couldn't; each time I began to nod off, the phone would ring and it would take me through it all over again.

I knew I'd better get up when I heard my sister slam the door to her room and start to replay the messages. She was always policing that stupid little machine, constantly nagging me to "answer the goddamn phone" so the machine wouldn't fill up and cut people off. But there was no incentive for me to do that. After all, it was her machine, her phone and her friends. And me, well, I was lucky enough to get the hand-me-down phone, the one where you had to hold the wires together just right to minimize the static and avoid hanging up on people midsentence.

I guess Carla was in a good mood that afternoon, because she didn't say a word to me until we sat down to dinner. Then as usual, she addressed me with a condescending edge to her voice as a reminder to me of our birth order.

"So this morning," she said with her mouth full of food, "who was the woman with the beak nose and the rosary around her neck?"

Leave it to Carla to call things as she saw them. The raw manner in which she conducted herself often put her at odds with our father, who found her, his firstborn daughter, a bit more outspoken than how he thought women ought to be.

"That was Sister Patrice Louvois," said my mother. "She's the assistant principal who came with Coach Krum. And I think that was a cross around her neck and not a rosary."

"Whatever. I'm just glad I'm not the one who has to stare at that every day," said Carla, pulling her thick, dark hair into a ponytail and then reaching over me for another tortilla. Cupping the tortilla in her hand, she piled on strips of beef with her fork. "Give me the guac," she barked, jabbing me with her elbow. I didn't feel like fighting, so I moved the bowl of guacamole in front of her plate. Just like a dog being told to sit.

"So I would think going to school with just girls would be so incredibly dull," she announced, spreading the green goop on her fajita. She turned to me. "*Güera*, are you really okay with that? I mean, not seeing guys all day?"

Before I could even begin to ponder my sister's question, my mother jumped in, apparently worried this could spark a fight—not from me, but from my father. He hated when Carla called me Güera, even though it was a harmless nickname that meant "white girl."

"Carla, your sister just isn't interested in boys yet like you," my mother said. "She's too busy with piano and basketball."

A devious grin spread across Carla's face. "Well, that's for sure," she said under her breath.

Carla's comment made me shift in my seat. I glanced at my father for some sort of reaction—a flash of his eyes, a clearing of his throat or perhaps just a disapproving grunt. But he appeared unmoved, keeping his eyes drawn to his plate. He was holding back from tearing into her. I could feel it.

Next to me, I could hear my sister grinding away at her food. She took another bite and turned to me again matter-of-factly.

"So tell me, Güera," she chided, slowing her speech to emphasize the Spanish pronunciation of my nickname. "Are you, like . . . gay or something?"

As usual and with everything, Carla went too far.

"Why do you say things like that?" I snapped, pushing away from the table. The chair's legs screeched against the tile.

"Carla, that's enough!" said my father and slammed his fist on the table. "You're done here. You can either shut your mouth or leave the table!"

In the wake of my father's outburst, a familiar look of panic spread across my mother's face. I could see her tensing up in the way she pulled her arms into her body and stiffened her shoulders. It had become an automatic reaction after years of living with my father's temper.

Carla, however, found great enjoyment in his anger. Unlike my mother and me, she wasn't afraid of my father and he knew it. She did her best to be everything he disapproved of or hated.

"Fine, I'll leave the table," Carla conceded with a smirk, obviously proud of herself for stirring things up. She stood up and narrowed her eyes in my direction. "It was just a question that I'm sure has crossed your minds at least once." She started toward her room, but my father called to her.

"Carla, stop and look at me."

My sister wheeled around, a "what now" expression on her face.

"To be pure of heart is to be pure of mind and body."

"Yeah, whatever you say, Dad," said Carla. She saluted him with a quick movement of her hand, and then turned to continue walking. My father stopped her again.

"Carla, I wasn't finished with you."

"Now what?"

"You will call your sister by her proper name."

This time Carla didn't answer as she turned on her heel and disappeared into the dark hallway that led to our bedrooms. A few seconds later, the door slammed to her room and her stereo erupted like a volcano from behind the walls. Much to my relief, my father let her go and went back to his supper.

I was left at the table with my mom and dad, who continued their meal in awkward silence. Sometimes it seemed like nobody in my family knew how to talk to each other without yelling or inflicting pain with the words spilling from our mouths. Carla had mastered this, and I believe it was out of pure meanness that she even suggested I was gay. But did she really know any better? What could we expect in a house of pain, littered with traps? It didn't matter how carefully you stepped or spoke, you'd eventually trip up and someone would get hurt.

Still, we were different, Carla and I, and we probably had been from the moment I was born. Unlike Carla, I didn't have my mother's dark skin or small frame. I was my father's child in every way—from our lily-white skin to our gangly limbs—except for my brown eyes, the only trait that connected me to my mother.

But I think it went beyond just physical appearance, for I gave my mother a terrible time when I was born. She told me I was too big to come out the normal way, so the doctor had to cut her open and pull me out. In the middle of it, my mother started hemorrhaging and then was in and out of consciousness for days. Because of this, we never got the chance to really develop the genuine closeness that normally occurs between a mother and baby in the first few days. Or maybe she was already too much in love with my older sister, whom she always described as her "petite six-pounder." "Just three pushes and she was out," my mother would say as she stood next to Carla and stroked her dark, silky mane. "Then she latched onto my breast as if we were made for each other." Usually at that point my sister would tell her how gross that was and storm out in disgust. Then I'd be stuck there, forced to listen to my mother recount how horrible my birth was and how she almost died giving me life.

My father's experience was quite different than that of my mother. For one thing, he missed my sister's birth altogether; the hospital tried reaching him, but he was away on his lunch hour. When he finally arrived at the hospital, he would tell me, my mother was so taken with Carla that "Louise barely knew I had even entered the room." Yes, my mother's name is Louise; well, really her name is Louisa, but my father had made it very clear that he preferred she go by Louise. I don't think he ever fully accepted that he married a Hispanic woman. Perhaps that's why my sister represented everything that was foreign to him—her feisty personality, her flirtatious manner and yes, even the dark pigment of her skin. Funny how Carla acted and even looked a lot like my Aunt Gina (you know, the one who gave me the nickname), and given the bad blood that had arisen between my father and Aunt Gina over the years, it's no surprise that Carla and our father were constantly at odds.

I, on the other hand, was a different story. While my coming into this world put a terrible strain on my mother's health—I was nearly ten pounds—I think it invigorated my father to see the sturdiness of my body and my pale skin, even if my light coloring earned me the nickname Güera from my aunt. He was forced to care for me during those first few days while my mother lay in the hospital, and when she finally came home after nearly a week, it was she who felt invisible as she looked on me for the first time, this oversized newborn who appeared so secure and natural in my father's arms. It was at that moment, she said to me years later, that she realized she had been nothing more than a medium for my entry into the world; that I was meant for my father and my father, for me.

That night at the table I sat there looking at my half-eaten fajita, not daring to raise my eyes to my parents or make any sudden moves that might set things off again. But I desperately needed to talk to them. I wanted to tell them that I was scared about switching schools and starting over on a new team. I wanted to tell them that I was thinking more and more about studying music—and not playing basketball—in college. I wanted to tell them that I felt like I didn't have a choice but to abide by their wishes, my father's wishes, borne out of his own dreams and failures. I wanted to tell them I'd lost my voice even before I had it, and if I ever got my fingers around it even for a second, I'd use it to tell them how much I desperately needed them to get along, how much I desperately thirsted for peace.

"I think I'm done," I said, losing my nerve. "I'd like to go to my room now."

"You've been in your room all day, Lauren," my father said. "Let's go out back and practice your jump shot."

Sensing my blue mood, my mother made a weak attempt to convince him otherwise. "Carl, not tonight. I think she's had enough for today."

My father chose to ignore my mother's comment completely, as he did with almost everything she said. He left the table and headed toward the garage, pausing only to ask if I was coming.

"There's not much daylight left, Lauren, and I'm not going to tell you twice."

Chapter 4

That night on the driveway, I missed nearly all the shots I took. I knew this probably infuriated my father, though he didn't entirely let his disgust for my clumsiness show. Instead he kept pacing back and forth with his arms resting on his midsection, shaking his head and making disapproving grunting noises when the basketball ricocheted off the rim with a clang.

"Concentrate, Lauren. Try again."

It was hopeless; my mind was elsewhere, still frozen at the kitchen table where the family dinner had collapsed. But my father continued to harp on me until well past dark. When I told him I could no longer see the basket, he flipped on the floodlight and then ordered me to tighten my high-tops. As I knelt on one knee to pull at my laces, out of the corner of my eye I saw him rub on his beard; a sign that he was close to coming unglued. It was obvious to me that he was in panic mode, probably terrified that he had promised Coach Krum too much. For someone who claimed to be a man of faith, it never took my father long to lose faith in me.

After many more failed attempts, I finally sank a few balls. This seemed to calm my father's nerves somewhat, though it didn't earn me any praise. He said we'd practice again tomorrow, and next time my head had better be on straight. At least he had figured one thing out—that something was bothering me—but that's as far as he went to acknowledge what might be wrong.

The issues I had with my father that night were nothing compared with what was really on my mind. The whole time I was out there throwing bricks against the backboard, all I could think about was June and how I'd be leaving her to become a big shot basketball player at Saint Agnes.

But I couldn't put off the call any longer. After showering and dodging a potentially nasty exchange with my sister, I dialed June's number and woke up her dad, who had no idea who I was for the first minute or so we were on the phone. His English wasn't always the best—especially when he was half-asleep.

"Who this?"

"Mr. Hui, it's Lauren. I'm sorry to be calling so late."

Silence. "Whah? Say again who this?"

"Mr. Hui, it's Lauren."

"Who?"

"Lauren Muchmore! Can I speak to June?"

"June? Call back lader."

Click. "Dad, I got it . . . Lauren?"

"Yeah, June. It's me."

"Whah? Who this?"

"Dad, I said I got it! Get off the phone!"

"I thought you told me you were going to turn off the ringer in your parents' room?"

"I did. They must have flipped it back on."

Silence.

"Dad, come on!"

Click.

"So where the hell have you been all day, Lauren? I called like fifty times."

"I know, I know. It's been a weird day."

"What's wrong?"

"Everything."

Click.

"Güera, get off the phone. I need to call Shakey."

"Carla, I just got on!"

"I said, get off the phone or I'll beat your ass!"

"June, I'll call you back."

As I sat there fuming while my sister giggled on the phone with her boyfriend, a heavy sense of shame wrapped its cold fingers around me. Here I was supposedly this gifted athlete who could score on almost anybody, yet I couldn't even stand up to my own sister. So how would I not fold at the slightest disappointment in June's voice? I replayed over in my mind what I would say to my friend, and decided that I'd have to handle my words very, very carefully to prevent June from thinking I was a sellout. She hated sellouts and so did I.

I guess the thought of disappointing her really got to me. She was the one person in my life who really understood me and accepted me for who I was. While she couldn't relate to my natural athletic ability or I to her bizarre obsession with science and math, we shared the same wacky sense of humor that had landed us in a fair amount of trouble over the years, though all in good fun. From appearance alone, you would think we went together like oil and water—me a lanky giant, she a petite Asian girl who took two strides for my every one. Nonetheless, we each had qualities that the other admired, and so our friendship came easily. We were kindred spirits, June and I, and the fact that we were spun from opposite spools didn't make a darn bit of difference.

When I finally talked to June that night, it was she who called back after calling over and over during my sister's two-hour phone call with Shakey. By this point it was well past midnight and I was trying my best not to nod off. Then my sister stormed into my room.

"That little bitch is on the phone for you."

"June?"

"Uh, yeah. It's not like anyone else calls you."

As I clambered to the phone, I couldn't help laughing at how June got under my sister's skin. Carla hated her as much as June hated her back, which now that I think about it, probably didn't help things between my sister and me. Apparently that night, June had kept calling every thirty minutes until Carla finally gave in.

"June?"

"My God, your sister's such a bitch!"

"Funny, she said the same thing about you."

Click.

"Shoot, she was still on the phone."

"Like I care. So what the hell is going on with you?"

At that point, the speech I had prepared pretty much went out the window. I stalled. I went in circles. I said everything I could to avoid breaking the bad news, but in the end I had to tell her the truth.

"You're *what*? Transferring to Saint Agnes?"

That was pretty much the reaction I had expected. She went on and on about how snobbish those girls were, and what in the world would she do without me?

"You know, I could take this a lot better if you told me your dad was getting transferred to Alaska or something. But Saint Agnes? I mean, come on, Lauren! Do you really want to be one of them?"

Wow, that one hurt. June knew I hated those girls, but still she had to go and say it. I heard her sigh on the other end of line. I knew she was frustrated that she couldn't quite figure out how it all worked in my family. June was no dummy; she knew something was off. But I couldn't bring myself to tell her just how warped my home life had become.

"Do you really think I have a choice in the matter? Of course I don't want to go to that fucking school!" Silence echoed on the line. I wasn't used to dropping the F-bomb.

"Well then, did you tell your parents that?"

Oh that June, she knew me way too well. No, I hadn't told them that. In fact, I had crumbled at their feet, or rather at my father's feet. He really was the orchestrator of all this, not my mother. As long as my father wasn't yelling, then my mother was happy—happy to be holed up in the living room, giving her piano lessons day after day to the dozen or so pupils that came under her instruction. At least those kids showed her some respect.

I had thought about going to my mother, about pleading with her to get me out of this mess, but it wouldn't have done any good. She'd have sided with my father, whether she truly agreed with the decision to send me to Saint Agnes or not. You would think she'd have had the motherly instinct to come to me, to check to make sure I was okay and not freaking out too much about transferring to a new school. But she never made it a point to do any of this; not even a reassuring squeeze to show that she at least halfway sensed my apprehension. I've long ago stopped being angry about my mother's indifference, because in those days there was no getting through to her. She moved through our house as a shell of herself, devoid of feeling and emotion, a robot programmed to serve her family under the dictatorship that was my father. The spirit of her true self, that beacon of light I saw twinkling behind her eyes in old photographs, had been lost somehow, or perhaps buried, along with her birth name, the day she and my father said "I do."

But how in the world could I express all of this to June when I barely understood it myself? I promised her that things wouldn't change, that we'd still talk every day and do things on the weekends. Sure, we wouldn't see each other at school anymore, but our schools were only a few miles apart. At least she could still take me and pick me up, like always.

"Damn, that means I'll be driving through enemy territory every day. I'll be eaten alive."

"Are you kidding me? I'm the one who has to go to school there!"

"True. I just don't want them changing you."

"Are you kidding? Who do you think you're talking to, me or Carla?"

When I finally got her laughing again, she told me that she was getting the raw end of the deal.

"How so?" I didn't have a clue where she was going with this.

"Think about it. I still have to go to school with your sister!"

I hadn't thought of that. "Oh yeah," I said. "Lucky you."

"Yeah, lucky me."

Chapter 5

There's really not much to say about my summer that year, other than the basketball camps I attended. Coach Krum always recommended that his players sign up for at least one or two, but for my father, that just wasn't enough. So I went to five, one of which was two weeks long and marked my first time on a college campus. The dorms were okay and the food was nasty, but I recall enjoying the Jello with whipped cream. Strange that the highlight of the camp was the dessert, but frankly, I was more than burned out on basketball by midsummer.

Not surprisingly, my piano studies slowly fell by the wayside. I was too tired to really practice all that much, and as for teaching, my mad basketball schedule began to conflict with young Ethan's lessons. That was the one thing I really didn't mind about all of this. Ethan's defiance toward me had worsened. During one of our last Saturday morning lessons, he threw himself violently to the floor and pitched a fit when I asked him to repeat "Send in the Clowns." I believe that particular lesson lasted a total of fifteen minutes, so I wouldn't say his mother was getting her money's worth. Was I really cut out to teach piano? I wondered that sometimes.

So toward the end of the summer, I was relieved when Coach Krum started holding open practices on Saturday mornings from nine to noon. Although they were voluntary, my father saw nothing optional about them, which meant my time with young Ethan would be no more; and good riddance, if you asked me.

You would think ridding myself of that little tyrant would have moved me to jump for joy. And it did for a time, right up to the point when my father announced his decision to attend the open practices. I must have looked at him like he was a disease that first Saturday morning, because he immediately went off on me about my attitude. Having him there was for my own good, and I'd thank him someday, and so on and so on. I don't remember the rest of the lecture. I was overcome with sheer embarrassment at what the other players would think, and we hadn't even set foot in the gymnasium yet.

To my surprise, only a handful of players showed up to that first practice. Coach Krum commended those of us who had and said we'd have a definite edge going into tryouts.

Wait a minute. Tryouts? You mean I don't have a guaranteed spot on this team?

That's when I started screaming. Not out loud, mind you, but inside my head. I couldn't believe that I was risking everything, I mean *everything*, to go play for stupid, stuck-up Saint Agnes, and I wasn't even officially on the team. That's all I could think about during that first practice, and because of that I couldn't sink a shot to save my life. My father was about to lose it. Here I was, fresh off five basketball camps, and I had lost all concept of how to dribble. The funny thing was that Coach Krum didn't really seem all that fazed, not even when my father walked me right up to him after the final whistle and made all sorts of excuses for why I had performed so badly. All Coach Krum said was "Relax, Mr. Muchmore. It's early."

But Mr. Muchmore couldn't relax. When we got home, he marched me straight out to the driveway and ordered me to shoot fifty free throws while I thought about what a poor excuse for a player I had become. I did what my father told me and sank a good number of them, mostly out of anger. But the hot Texas sun bore down on my forehead, making my glasses slip from all the sweat beads dripping down my face.

I got so hot that at one point I was afraid I'd pass out. About the time I started to see spots and had to lean my head over on my knees, my mother came rushing outside and pleaded with my father to stop this nonsense. I could still hear them hollering at each other out on the driveway even after I had run inside and slammed the door to my room. The only way I knew to drown out their fighting was to turn the shower on, so I did. I was filthy anyway.

June didn't say much on the phone that afternoon when I told her I couldn't go to the movies like we had planned. I explained what had happened at practice, but I didn't go into the rest of it. The truth was that I hadn't asked to go to the movies in the first place, because I knew if I did, it would disrupt the quiet calm that had finally settled on the house. I told June that I was grounded, though I hadn't received any punishment. Maybe I was just trying to keep the peace; but maybe it was my way of punishing myself for performing so poorly at practice and for causing the terrible exchange of words that had erupted between my mom and dad that day.

June suggested she could just come over, but I was quick to discourage that, too. I couldn't risk her witnessing a violent outburst from my parents. June and I were close, but we weren't that close.

It's not that I didn't trust her, because I would have trusted her with my life. It was just that I wasn't yet comfortable divulging all that went on in my family. I had done a pretty good job over the years brushing over it, and I figured I'd keep up the charade as long as I could. We spent most of our time over at June's house anyway because of my sister, or at least that's what I wanted her to believe. Plus I loved it over at the Huis'. I got to eat homemade shrimp dumplings, authentic noodle dishes and as many fruit tarts and crepes as I wanted.

June's father was the total opposite of mine. Aside from being an amazing cook, Franklin Hui wore a smile that started with his eyes and radiated across his entire face. June's mother, Monique, was eccentric and loud and would pull you in with her thick French accent and then linger with you for hours through the lavender scent she'd leave on your clothes. Although Franklin and Monique came from contrasting cultures and backgrounds, they melted together as if they were made from the same mold, unlike my parents, who seemed to loathe the very breath of the other. My parents both grew up in Texas, but you'd think they came from opposite ends of the world. My dad's first visit to South Texas, or what folks like to call the Valley, came shortly after he and my mother were engaged. Four hours into that first visit, he got into a brawl with one of my mom's cousins, who called him a gringo. What her cousin had intended as playful teasing, my father took as a racial insult. The more my mom tried convincing him that her cousin had meant no harm, the deeper my dad dug his heels into the ground. My dad demanded they leave immediately and drove the eight hours all the way back to Dallas. He returned to the Valley only one more time after that: for my *abuela*'s funeral. I remember that at one point during the rosary, as I listened to my mom recite the Lord's Prayer in Spanish, I could have sworn I heard my dad mumble "wetbacks" under his breath.

The atmosphere that my parent's history created was just too heavy for June's world. Mine too, if I'm really honest with myself. But in those days it was all about survival, and I didn't want to do or say anything that would scare June off. Admitting to her how unsafe I felt in my own home was too big of a burden to unravel at her feet, and I couldn't risk her parents finding out. So I quickly changed the subject and said I'd call her before bed. But before we got off the phone, June asked me a question that stopped me cold. "So, what do you think of him?"

"Of who?" I said.

"Your coach! What do you think of your new coach?"

"Oh, him. He's okay, I guess. Why?"

"I just wondered, since you're switching schools to go play for him and all. I mean, everyone knows he's some big hotshot."

For a split second I debated telling June that I didn't have a guaranteed spot on the team, and if I flubbed it during tryouts, I was pretty much up a creek. But just as quickly as the thought crossed my mind, I did away with it. I didn't need another lecture, even if it was from my friend. So instead I spoke the first thing that fell from my mouth: "Well, his legs are hairy."

June paused a moment or two before posing her next question. "Is he cute?"

"I don't know. He's like thirty-five or something."

"Well, he sounds pretty boring to me."

"Yeah, we'll see. Can't really tell yet, but I'm hoping he's cool. The last thing I need is a jerk for a coach."

"True, because you already have plenty of those."

"Coaches?"

"No, jerks."

From June's comment, I realized that she probably had picked up on more of the issues with my family than I had led myself to believe. I chose to leave it be, even though she had left the door wide open, because my head was pounding and I wanted to forget how screwed up things were most of the time. After I hung up with June, I ventured into the kitchen, where I traced the phone cord along the vinyl flooring to the walk-in pantry. A light spilled out from under the closed door. Then a familiar whiff of smoke hit me and I figured that my mother was probably smoking a cigarette and talking on the home line with her sister Gina—two things my father despised.

An hour or so earlier, I had heard the rattle of the garage door and the sound of a car pulling away. I had assumed it was my father leaving for the evening; he always disappeared for a few hours after a fight with my mom. One time, after a particularly intense confrontation, my sister had followed him, curious about where he was venturing. Turns out she found him at church, in the chapel, kneeling in front of the Blessed Sacrament. According to Carla, who had snuck in from the back to spy on him, he appeared to be deep in prayer, his hands clasped together and his head resting on the pew in front of him. When she told me this, I'll admit my disdain for him softened a little. It would have been easier for me to hate my father if Carla had found him at a bar, drowning himself in whiskey or pawing over some ninny. I wondered, though, what he was praying for. What was he asking of God? Was he begging the Lord to help him control his anger? Was he asking for forgiveness for hitting my mother? Or was he asking that God bring obedience to his wife and daughters? One would never know, but I'd probably vote for the latter.

With my father out of the house that night, I felt drawn to the piano. So I made myself a peanut butter and jelly sandwich and went to the living room. My fingers felt sticky when I started to play, but I didn't fret about smudging strawberry jam on the keys. I had grown tired of worrying. All I wanted to do was let the rhythm of the music ebb and flow through me.

I began playing my favorite, "Clair de lune." There was something about the piece that always soothed me, with its unlikely pauses and the arresting way in which the crescendo would build. I played it slowly that night, not wanting to reach the end. The notes were really quite lovely, and although I made one or two minor blunders on the keys, I didn't let this stop me. I played right over my missteps and pretended I was performing in a vast recital hall. There, in my make-believe place, I was a concert pianist, conjuring up sounds so rich and sweet that even my father couldn't deny their reverent beauty. At last, though, I came to the end of the piece and with a weight on my shoulders, played the final chord.

It was then that I realized my mother was curled up on the settee behind me. Her eyes looked red and weepy, a sign that she'd been crying. She coughed a little before she spoke, and she looked at me with eyes I also knew to be mine.

"I miss your playing, Güera."

She called me Güera—the very nickname my father hated. I assumed she said what she did to show me affection, to remind me that she too had a part in my life and that my skin would never be as white as my father might hope it would be.

"I miss it, too."

A tired smile spread across her face. "Your Aunt Gina asked about you . . . wanted to make sure that you're still practicing the piano."

"When I can, of course," I said, wanting so badly to unload on her everything that was bothering me. Though that night I wouldn't be so lucky.

"I think I'll go to bed now," she said. "It's been a long day." But instead of getting up and immediately walking out of the living room, she sat there with her fist to her mouth as if she had more to say. I thought maybe she was preparing to speak, but she brushed a wisp of black hair behind her ears. Her cheek glowed from a slap of a hand.

"Mom, your face."

She immediately tilted her head so that her shoulder-length hair fell forward to cover the bruise.

"It's nothing. I bumped it on the door. I'm so clumsy."

I had heard that excuse a hundred times before: she had bumped her head getting groceries out of the car or cut her lip in the shower on the door handle while shaving. When I was little, I used to believe these stories without question, but I wasn't little anymore. I knew better. Sitting there that night watching my mother fidget with her hair, I tried to think of something to say, something that would get her to open up to me. But I couldn't find the words to make her stay seated long enough.

"I can play another song," I said, hoping my offer of music would entice her to stay with me awhile longer. I felt responsible for the fighting that afternoon—fighting that had led to her swollen face—and I wanted to make up for it.

My mother rose slowly from the sofa. "Yes, that would make me happy, baby, but I'm much too tired." She looked back at me, careful not to turn the swollen side of her face in my direction. "Tomorrow, baby, if your father's in a good mood."

Chapter 6

There were not many people who could put my father in his place. My sister probably came the closest to doing it, bowing up to him like some kind of street fighter, taunting him to "go ahead and hit me" when their yelling matches got out of hand. I watched him raise his fist to her on a number of occasions. Surprisingly, he never struck her; perhaps he feared that if he did, he wouldn't be able to stop himself from beating her to death. By the time Carla was seventeen, though, our father's outbursts over her disobedience had become less frequent, even when she stayed out all night. I suspect that he had grown tired of trying to mold her into a God-fearing individual, eventually throwing up his hands at her behavior.

Because he considered his firstborn daughter lost to the ways of sin, there was nothing left for my father to do but turn his attention to me. This unwavering focus grew into a heavy burden, one that I feared would bear down on me for the rest of my life. It was much to my relief, then, that Coach Krum put his arm around my father at the beginning of the next practice and slowly escorted him out of the gym. I don't know what the coach said to him that morning, but my father never sat in on any of my practices from that day forward. I guessed that Coach Krum had told him in a friendly way to get going; he'd take things from there. Whatever words he used, they left my father at ease and me grateful.

On the heels of my father's departure, my knack for dribbling and shooting seemed to return, not only on that Saturday but on those that followed as well. Over the next several weeks, a few more players showed up, most of them incoming freshmen. Coach Krum pretty much let us do what we wanted during those summer practices. If we were tired, he didn't care if we rested or even if we cut out of practice early. He spent most of the time observing us from the stage, propped up on an elbow, scribbling on a notepad. From time to time he'd look up from his notebook and grin at someone's jump shot or drive to the basket. Whenever I made a particularly smart play, like stealing a ball or maneuvering between two defenders for an easy layup, I'd look over in his direction to make sure he was watching. But mostly his head would be buried in his notebook or he'd have disappeared into his office in the back of the weight room. This frustrated me. I felt the need to prove myself to him, because if I didn't make the team, I knew my dad would certainly have my hide.

I guess I was motivated mostly by fear and (okay, I'll admit it) a little by my own need to impress. I mean, come on, who wouldn't want to make an impact on someone like Daniel Krum? He was young and successful and a winner. Whenever I'd notice him looking even remotely in my direction, I'd turn on the hustle and prey upon the weaker players whom I knew would never make the cut, chopping them up and exploiting their shortcomings one by one.

My big-headedness on the basketball court evaporated the day a burly-looking brute of player named Beth Polanski showed up. I placed her immediately as the team's ruling point guard—one of the players who had caused me tremendous grief during that infamous Saint Agnes game. How I'd forgotten about her was beyond me, but as soon as I saw her go up to the coach and give him a great big bear hug as if he were an old college buddy, I felt a swell of jealousy and my ego shrank down to nothing. In fact, I was a nothing—nothing more than a stupid transfer looking even stupider when I slammed into a defender, and then had to crawl on my hands and knees to feel around for the glasses that had flown off my face.

God, I hated having to wear those things, and that day I hated them even more when it was Beth who found them. She came bounding over like King Kong and lowered to one knee for an eye-level look at me on the floor.

"Looking for these?" she said, extending the glasses in front of me.

Yes, you big ugly boar, I'm looking for those. Now take your grubby hands off of them and go stuff your fat ass back under the gigantic rock you managed to squeeze out from. So maybe I didn't say those exact words, but I sure as hell was thinking them.

"Thanks."

That's all I could say. *Thanks.* Words always failed me whenever I got a case of the nerves. The rest of the players formed a circle around us, though most of their eyes were fixed on me. The skin on my neck prickled, followed by a burning sensation, which meant my neck had turned beet red.

"I'm Beth Polanski. Nice to meet ya."

Shit. I'd thought she'd graduated.

"Coach tells me you're coming to us from Pius."

"Yeah."

Beth offered her hand. I grabbed it and she yanked me up off the ground.

"What's your name?"

"Lauren. Lauren Muchmore."

"Oh yeah, that's right. The one from last season's game."

Damn her for remembering.

"Tough crowd, but I doubt anyone will remember you. Well, come on, Muchmore, let's see whatcha got."

I was astounded at how much Beth Polanski reminded me of a boy. There was nothing feminine about her except for the shell and hemp necklace tied around her neck, and even that was questionable. She wore her jet-black hair cropped at the ears, which reminded me of the chili-bowl cut I had once as a kid. She must have just returned from the beach (or else her family had a swimming pool), because she was tanned a golden brown. You would think that the extra weight she packed on would have slowed her down, but on the court she moved in a fluid motion and had the ball-handling skills of a pro.

When you scored a bucket, she'd pat you on the butt, and if you missed a free throw, she'd pat you on the butt all the same and say, "Nice try there, sport." And it wasn't long before I found myself growing fond of Beth and appreciative of having a teammate like her around. She took me under her wing in a way, feeding me the inside scoop on everything, including where she thought "Coach," as she referred to him, would place people.

"Coach and I've been talking, Muchmore, and I'm sure it won't be long before he'll start you at two."

The *two* she was referring to was the number two guard position; the wingman, so to speak, to the point guard, a position which Beth was very clear in stating belonged to her.

"We lost a lot of our seniors who were heavy hitters down low, so it'll be our job to keep things moving at the point. Don't know what Coach will do when I graduate next year, but I suppose that's why he's brought you on board. It'll be important to stick close to me so I can train you on the point position, because it'll be up to you to step in next year. I'll be sure to write."

Step in next year? I must have missed something, because I had been under the impression I was to step in *this* year. But I figured Beth knew what she was talking about, being a senior and all, and so I decided to keep my focus on getting through tryouts and the other hurdle in my life—surviving the first week at a brand new school when all eyes would be checking out the new girl.

To make matters worse, my mom had left the hem of my uniform skirt way too long (it hung past my knees) and she told me she wouldn't have enough time to redo it before I stepped into the halls of Saint Agnes. Carla must have heard our fussing that morning, because she waltzed right up to me with her uniform skirt on—the one hemmed a good length *above* the knees—and asked me if *Little House on the Prairie* skirts were the in thing at Saint Agnes. Usually I could handle Carla's comments without blowing my top, but that day I'm not sure what got into me. Carla's ribbing finally pushed me to the boiling point. Before I really knew what I was doing, Carla was tumbling over the toilet into the tub, legs flailing around and her backside in full view.

Wouldn't have been the first time.

Luckily for me the shower curtain slowed her fall, or else she might have hit the back of her head on the porcelain. Hmm . . . on second thought, that might not have been such a bad thing, given the symphony of expletives that rang out from her mouth: "You fucking bitch . . . You're nothing but a freak . . . You're just like Dad . . . If you ever touch me again, I'll kill you ..." and so on and so on. My cue to leave came when I heard Carla tattling to our mom in the kitchen about how I'd tried to kill her, and was she just going to stand there and let me get away with it? I didn't want to stick around to find out. I grabbed my bags and walked out to the driveway to wait for June, and just as I got to the curb, I saw her black Ford Bronco emerge over the hill. I sighed in relief.

"Tough morning?"

"You have no idea."

Sitting in the passenger seat next to June, there was no avoiding the fact that we now went to rival schools. We still wore uniform skirts—both lay flat from the waist, with pleats flaring out from the top of the thighs—but the colors clashed unmistakably now, hers the more familiar dark green and gray plaid and mine a medley of green, yellow, white and brown. We each had on white short-sleeved blouse, though with one distinct difference. Mine had the official Saint Agnes crest on the pocket, and very soon I'd come to learn more about that darn little crest than I ever would want to know.

Saint Agnes students had the choice of wearing two kinds of shoes, either the brown penny loafer or the black and white saddle shoe. I chose the latter because that's what I'd worn at Pius, and my old pair seemed to be in good enough shape. I wasn't quite sure about the squiggly designs etched in blue ink on the white leather tops, but I was willing to risk it rather than ask my parents for a new pair. The dress code also required a dark green blazer, emblazoned, of course, with the Saint Agnes crest. Since it was still so hot outside, I decided to leave it home that first day, thinking that I really wouldn't need it. More importantly, June had let me borrow one of her Swatches—the big clear one with the gears—and I didn't want it covered up.

Oh God, why did I have to be so vain.

As I came to find out rather quickly that morning, blazers were required to be worn to class, from class and to all school assemblies. Once again I stuck out like a fresh pimple, blazer-less and in my *Little House on the Prairie* skirt, looking like an idiot while maneuvering through a sea of schoolgirls along the main hallway.

Obviously my watch was slow because as I rounded the corner for one more pass down the main hall, I saw a boney, birdlike woman emerge from the front office. She had the longest neck I'd ever seen in my life. She could have gone head to head with a crane in a neck wrestling contest and come out the winner. She even looked like a bird by the way wore her hair; short, feathered and covering her ears. And her nose could have come straight from the Wicked Witch in *The Wizard of Oz*, because of the large and protruding crick that edged out from its bridge.

Then I spotted what my sister had referred to as the "rosary" hanging around her neck, and it occurred to me that this woman standing a yard or two away from me, this woman looking down at her watch with a furrowed brow, might have at one time paid a visit to my home.

"Sixty seconds, ladies. You have less than a minute to find your rooms."

Yup. Same pitchy voice that sounded like a squawking bird. Undeniably, it was Sister Patrice Louvois. Good, I thought. I'd ask her to direct me to Sillaway Theatre, where sophomore orientation was a mere five minutes from starting. I did, and the conversation went something like this:

"Can you please tell me where Sillaway Theatre is?"

"Rather late for directions, don't you think?"

"Well, I'm new here, you know . . . my first day."

"And you are?"

"Lauren Muchmore."

"Oh yes, Lauren. I came to your house, but you were too busy to properly introduce yourself." As she said this she folded her arms and began to rock back and forth on the balls of her feet. I got the feeling that she was gearing up for a lecture and would enjoy every moment of it.

"All transfers received detailed maps and instructions for start of school events and requirements," she said pointedly, inspecting my uniform down the length of my body and stopping abruptly at my feet. "Is that marker drawings on your shoes?"

"I must have left them at home."

"Your shoes?"

"No, I'm sorry, the maps. I accidentally forgot the maps."

"Well, that's unacceptable!"

I jumped when the bell rang.

"Well, it looks like we'll have more time to discuss your lack of preparedness, among other things, while I write you a tardy slip."

I had never expected to visit the assistant principal's office so soon into my career at Saint Agnes. I already felt like a failure, and it was only a minute or two past eight o'clock. As I watched Sister Louvois scribble away on a pink slip of paper, I racked my brain for something to say that would communicate how sorry I was for being such an idiot.

"Sister?"

She kept on writing and wouldn't look at me. Her silence cut into me.

"Sister Louvois?"

"I heard you the first time, Miss Muchmore," she said, without drawing her eyes away from the tardy slip. As I watched her move the pen across the pink paper in precise loops and slants, I couldn't help fixing my eyes on her boney hands. Her fingers stuck out of her palms like bamboo, with tufts of dry, flaky skin at the knuckles. I likened them in my mind to the scaly membrane of a bird. Sister Patrice Louvois, the bird woman.

Before I could congratulate myself on my vivid imagination, her crooked nose was again pointing in my direction. "You had something to say?"

"I just wanted to apologize for being unprepared and late."

"Who takes you to school?"

"Excuse me?"

"It's a simple question, don't you think?"

"Well, my friend . . . um."

"A friend?"

"Yes, my friend June. She goes to Pope Pius."

"A former classmate, I take it."

"Sometimes I get a ride with my sister. She also goes to Pius."

"But *you* don't anymore, so I suggest you have a talk with your friend and your sister to make sure you arrive here on time."

"Yes, Sister."

"Now, you better hurry yourself to the assembly before you miss out on anything more."

Sister Louvois seemed to soften a bit, voluntarily escorting me to Sillaway Theatre and pointing out different parts of the school along the way. I remember her moving with considerable purpose, her arms swinging at her side as she led our promenade with her nose. As I trotted beside her, I got the feeling she was a woman of little patience—one who believed that everything had its place. Several times she stopped in her tracks to straighten one of the hundreds of graduation portraits lining the walls, or to scoop up a stray gum wrapper from the floor. When we finally arrived at our destination, she quickly did away with the niceties and resumed herself as the bird woman.

"Please be advised that two more tardies will land you in detention. Six thirty to eight o'clock."

She turned and left me standing in front of two broad oak doors. My eyes set upon a gold-plated sign that read Sillaway Theatre in large script lettering. I stood there for a moment, trying to draw up the nerve to go inside. I think I was still reeling from my run-in with Sister Louvois. And that's when I saw it, a vision of that bird woman standing next to my sister, both donning matching black pointy hats and then zooming off together on their brooms. I giggled, took a deep breath and pulled open the heavy wooden doors.

Chapter 7

You would think that the first day at a new school would be an overload of policy and procedures, faculty introductions, class schedules and so forth. That was pretty much the program for most of the morning, but after lunch the gears quickly shifted as I, together with about six hundred other plaid-skirted girls, shuffled into the main hall for First Mass. Father Glen, a priest from the neighboring all-boys school, graciously said Mass for us girls as a handful of nuns (some of them looking a year or so younger than God) and the rest of the faculty sat in the front three rows. So did Coach Krum, who I noticed had shaved his mustache. After a short homily, Father Glen handed the pulpit over to the principal of Saint Agnes—Dr. Blanche Rainey—who allegedly had left the nunhood many years before, or at least that's what the girl next to me said.

Dr. Rainey stood at least six feet tall and wore a drab navy suit that hung loosely on her husky frame. Her booming voice and the way she talked with her hands captured my full attention. I could see why she was the school's principal from the way she commanded the room, turning to face all angles of the main hall as if addressing each student personally.

What she said was all very interesting. The entire premise for the school was based on the life of a young girl named Agnes, a fourth-century Christian girl who met an untimely death at the age of twelve. Dr. Rainey went on to say that Agnes was considered one of four great *virgin* martyrs of the Christian Church and that we all should fashion ourselves by Agnes's example. As the story goes, young Agnes made it known that she wished to stay—and I quote—"a virgin in Christ" by refusing to marry the son of a Roman prefect. The problem, if I understood Dr. Rainey, was that Agnes's outright devotion to her faith happened to occur during the reign of Diocletian, the Roman emperor who ordered the last great persecution of Christians. And so it was that she was put to death, and in her death she became known as the patron saint of young women and the protectress of bodily purity, making her one of the most widely honored Roman martyrs and Christian saints of her day.

Fashion ourselves by Agnes's example. This idea churned in my head as Dr. Rainey went on to explain for the new students—and to review ad nauseam for the veterans—the virtues of Saint Agnes on which the school was founded.

PEACE PURITY SACRIFICE

Behind Dr. Rainey hung three massive green banners showcasing each virtue and its corresponding symbol. I studied them intently—thinking we might be tested—looking from one to the other as Dr. Rainey took us through their meanings. It was all very simple, really. For *peace* there was a white dove; given its universal meaning, no surprise there. *Purity* was a no-brainer as well, represented by an angel with clasped hands. And finally there was *sacrifice*, defined by a plain white cross that obviously symbolized the death of Christ.

Even as a fifteen-year-old, I knew what they were trying to impress upon us. Let's see. Peace meant don't question authority, and do what you're told. Purity, don't have sex. Sacrifice, put others first and don't complain. Lesson over.

I know I sound a bit jaded, but these are some pretty high expectations to live up to, especially when you're an impressionable teenage girl. If you're told enough times that this is how you should behave, then you begin to believe that living your life any other way will damn you to hell. But I knew as I sat there listening to Dr. Rainey that they wouldn't have to worry about me, because I was as straitlaced as they came. If my parents gave me a curfew of ten o'clock, I'd arrive at a quarter to ten. If I happened upon a twenty-dollar bill, I'd go around asking who dropped it. And how many times had I reminded June that my parents wouldn't allow me to watch R-rated movies?

My sister Carla, though, was another story. I figured she probably wouldn't last five minutes at my new school. The second she heard that Agnes had died a virgin, she'd be out the door in a flash, not wanting to suffer the same fate (dying a virgin, that is, not the dying itself). But not me; I was content to be the good girl, because that was the only way I knew to live.

This might sound odd, but I actually came to appreciate Dr. Rainey's lecture on Agnes and the background of the school. For one thing, I finally understood the meaning of the crest branded on the front pocket of our blazers (which, if you recall, I had left at home). Similar to a Girl Scout badge, the emblem featured each virtue's symbols in white, superimposed on a light brown background. Across the top in crimson script lettering read Saint Agnes School, with the date of the school's founding—1882—at the bottom.

I quickly learned something else: seniors wore pale yellow blouses and white blazers, so it was easy to pick them out from the sea of schoolgirls. Instinctively, I made every attempt to avoid them, because I'd already gotten myself into enough trouble that first day. But come lunchtime, as I stood in the cafeteria holding my tray and looking like what I'm sure seemed a complete idiot, my strategy failed miserably when Beth Polanski waved me over—no, make that *heckled* me over. When she spotted me looking around for a seat in the crowded room, she—no lie—stood up on her chair and shouted my name.

"Hey, Muchmore! Muchmore! Get over here!"

I looked over and saw her waving her arms in the air. More and more students were starting to look my way. All I wanted her to do was shut up, so I quickly walked toward her table, which to my distress was stocked entirely with seniors staring up at me.

"Hey," I said, trying to wave and hold my tray at the same time.

"That food is total crap," Beth said, yanking the tray out of my hands. "Here, have some pizza."

Sprawled in the middle of the table were several open pizza boxes with every kind of pie imaginable. "We ordered them just before lunch," she said. "Louvois hates when we do this, but we don't give it any bother."

As if she hadn't already drawn enough attention to me, she proceeded to bark at the girls sitting one table over to give her their empty chair, and then dragged it across the floor to our table.

"Here, sit next to Vines. She's on the team too."

I sat back on the chair harder than I would have liked. The girl next to gave me a nod as she tore at another slice of pizza. I noticed she wore unlaced high-tops, which looked as big as my father's sneakers. I looked around and then sank a little in my seat; I didn't want a teacher seeing me associating with someone who wasn't following the dress code. And then I realized that the person breaking the rules was Emerson Vines, the center I'd managed to score on only a couple times the previous year. She was tough to get around, that's for sure.

"So what year are you?" someone asked.

Not knowing who was talking, I squared my gaze on the pizza boxes. "Sophomore."

"Muchmore came to us from Pius."

"My condolences," someone said. A round of snickers followed.

Emerson shifted toward me. "Wait, I think I remember you . . . you're that guard, right?"

I wasn't sure what she meant by "that guard," so I just shrugged.

"Yeah, I guess."

"Muchmore's gonna be my number two," said Beth. "Coach's gotta do something for when we leave." Everyone seemed to nod in agreement at Beth's point, and soon after, to my relief, the conversation about basketball tapered off. I sat there the rest of the lunch period, not saying a word and not really eating much, either—something I still do when I get nervous.

By two o'clock, I was starving and still had the prospect of tryouts to consider, so when the final bell rang that afternoon, I made a beeline to the vending machines and scraped together enough change for some snack crackers and a soda, hoping they would give me enough energy to turn my game on.

They say the caffeine buzz wears off pretty quickly, but that afternoon I think the soda stayed with me all the way until six o'clock. Call it adrenaline or a case of nerves; I was unstoppable, having one of my best days on the court in a long while. There was no shot I could miss or rebound I couldn't snag. For a moment I caught myself actually hoping my father would turn up to watch. I ran circles around everyone, including the seniors I had lunched with earlier. Beth, I could tell, was thoroughly impressed, as she commented several times that "Muchmore came to play."

I know you're wondering about Coach Krum, and so was I during tryout week. He didn't say much, just told us to break up into groups and scrimmage. He'd blow the whistle to start play but wouldn't really say anything else. I did notice, though, that he now carried a clipboard as he strolled around the gym watching us. Occasionally he'd pause and scribble a note or two with a short stubby pencil or crouch low to the floor for a better angle at a play. I'll admit this rattled my nerves some, watching him record the good plays, the bad plays and the downright ugly ones. I wasn't about to get a mark by my name, so I turned up my game even more, so much so that at one point I found myself wrestling on the ground for a loose ball with Emerson Vines. For a minute there I thought I had ripped her head off when I tore the ball out of her grip. She shot up off the ground and thrust her hands into my chest, making me fall backward and lose my glasses.

"What's your problem? This isn't the championship!" she said. Beth, of course, trotted over to Emerson, threw her arms around her and told her to cool her head. The whole time, Coach Krum just stood there and watched, not intervening or saying a word, but as I pulled myself up off the ground and repositioned my specs on my nose, I could have sworn I saw a grin on his face.

Over the next three days, I continued to smoke everyone who dared stand up to me. Coach eventually paired Beth and me together on the same team, and our chemistry seemed to work well. I'd throw in the ball to her and she'd work it down the court. As her number two, I stuck to my job, dishing the ball out and getting open. But a few times I allowed myself to be selfish and took the jump shot or went for an easy layup on my own. Beth might have been a bit bothered by this, given that her customary slap on the rear didn't carry its usual vigor.

The week flew by and before I knew it, Friday was upon me. It was the last day of tryouts and I felt pretty good about making the team. We dressed out as usual (me opting to change clothes in the girls' restroom) and made our way into the gym. But this time, Coach Krum was nowhere to be found. Instead, tacked to the bulletin board outside the weight room was a sheet of paper with twelve names typed on it, including positions.

Lady Lambs Varsity Basketball Team

Arnold, Dashawn (G)

Bergstrom, Sonja (F)

Delcambre, Julie (F)

Hardman, D'Ana (F)

Karringan, Kristy (F)

Lohr, Tracey (F)

Muchmore, Lauren (G)

Oglesforth, Lynn (G)

Pauley, Page (C)

Polanski, Beth (G)

Tandy, Jennifer (C)

Vines, Emerson (C)

Seeing my name on the list brought a rush of relief. Beth came up behind me, hooked her arm around my neck and ruffled my hair. A few of the other girls were pumping their fists in the air in celebration, while some were still trying to jockey in close enough to scour the list of names. Most of the girls had examined the list by the time Coach Krum appeared from the weight room, swabbing his face and neck with a towel. His Saint Agnes T-shirt had rings of sweat under each arm, and his face looked flushed. The chatter in the gym simmered down as he made his way through the crowd of girls and told us to sit on the floor because he had a few things to say. I looked around and saw that some of the girls had red and blotchy eyes, and I couldn't understand why they were still hanging around. If my name had been absent from the list, I'd have broken into a full run out the door.

"Just because your name's not on the list doesn't mean you didn't give me your best this past week," Coach Krum began, hiking his leg over a stray folding chair. "I saw a lot of effort this week, and for that, I thank each and every one of you. But since we don't have a junior varsity, it makes this a whole lot harder. I wish I could've taken more of you . . . but I just can't."

He paused for a moment, stepping off the chair and moving away from it. "If any of you have questions as to why your name's not on the list, I'd be glad to sit down with you and give my assessment. I believe it's important, and only fair, that you fully understand the reasons for it if you so wish. Just schedule some time during my regular office hours and we can talk."

I was struck by his offer to speak with those who were cut. I wasn't used to this sort of openness. But I appreciated it for the sake of the girls he had cut, as I was sure they were finding it hard to quell the lump in their throats.

"I hope you will continue to come out and support us in the coming season," he said. "Just because you're not on this team doesn't mean we don't need you to cheer us on. So I want to thank you again for your efforts, and I wish you all the best of luck."

Silence fell on us as Coach Krum stood there and waited. A couple of the girls started to get up, realizing that he had just bid them goodbye. Others looked around, puzzled. Krum quickly picked up on their confusion, and asked the new team members to remain seated.

He waited until the last girl had left the gymnasium before he addressed us as the new varsity team. He offered his congratulations, of course, but made it a point of asking that we carry this honor reverently, reminding us of the girls who had just left. He told us that making the team was one thing, but pulling off a winning season was quite another. "We have a particularly challenging season ahead of us," he said. "We have the opportunity to break a school record of three consecutive district titles, and prove wrong those who think it can't be done. There's a lot expected of us and that means we've got to work even harder."

I absorbed the meaning of his words and wondered if I was good enough.

"You're here because you have potential, but that doesn't necessarily make you good. If you want to get better and be a part of this school's history, then I need you to give me everything. Because anything short of that just won't do."

Every pair of eyes, including my own, was glued on Daniel Krum. He let a minute pass as he paced slowly in front of us, rubbing his clean-shaven chin. Then finally he congratulated us again and told us to enjoy the long weekend.

"I'll see you all at 3:45 sharp on Tuesday afternoon. Don't be late."

Chapter 8

I hadn't planned on being done with tryouts so early that afternoon, so I called June from the pay phone outside the cafeteria, hoping she could pick me up early. I knew my mom probably had piano lessons scheduled past six, and I didn't dare call my sister. I'd managed to dodge Carla the entire week after our rumble by getting up extra-early to shower before she woke and spending most of the evenings in my room. I wasn't about to go and mess that all up.

But I still ended up doing a really stupid thing. After calling June to pick me up, I was waiting outside the gym when Beth and Emerson drove through the parking lot in Beth's Jeep. Seeing me, Beth stopped and offered me a ride.

"I'm waiting for a friend," I said over the music blaring from Beth's stereo. Emerson stared at me blankly from the passenger seat, her hand clutching the Jeep's railing. I knew she could probably not care less if I rode with them or not.

"Suit yourself, but I wouldn't want to be stuck here on a Friday."

Beth had a point, and June was running late. I was sure she'd understand. I mean, how could she blame me for wanting to make friends and fit in? With that rationale in my head, I hopped in the back of Beth's Jeep and we were off with a jolt as the back tires squealed against the pavement.

August's hot, dry wind whipped my ponytail as we rode along. I felt as if I was on the edge of coolness as I watched Emerson bob her head up and down to the REM song blasting from the speakers. Beth whipped the Jeep in and out of traffic and I clutched the crossrails to steady myself. For the first time I had a sense of what it felt like to be popular. Here I was riding along in the backseat of a Jeep with two seniors from Saint Agnes, and it was making me feel good, proud that I could hang with this kind of lot.

We came to an abrupt stop at a light and an older woman in a sedan looked up at us, frowned and quickly shifted her eyes away. The light turned green and Beth hit the gas, blasting out into the intersection and weaving across three lanes. The next song on the cassette came on and she turned it up even louder while making a sharp left turn that almost ejected me out of my seat.

When we arrived at my house, though, my stomach dropped at the sight of my Aunt Gina's clunker parked in the driveway. Not only was her shoddy 1970 El Camino an eyesore, with its faded blue paint and leaky oil, but I knew that her presence would spark a fight—a big one—the second my father walked through the door. I rolled my eyes at the four cars jammed in our driveway: my mom's station wagon, my sister's Pontiac, Shakey's Integra and of course Gina's piece of shit. Well this was lovely. Beth and Emerson probably thought we operated a junkyard. But there was nothing I could do about that, and I figured I had worse things to worry about, like how to keep the peace. Neither Beth nor Emerson budged from their seats, so I decided to exit the Jeep the way I had come in—by jumping off the back.

I had maybe taken two steps from the Jeep when Beth yelled, "See ya later!" and peeled off down my street. Walking across the yard, I could already hear the melody of a spirited *cumbia* pumping from the house. Were they crazy? Not only was Gina not welcome when my father was around but he had little tolerance for Tejano music either and preferred that my mother not play it in his presence. And if those two things weren't enough to get him in a bad mood (which I seriously doubted), then the sight of my sister's boyfriend Shakey, whom he

considered nothing less than a sleaze, would certainly push him
to the breaking point.

As I shut the front door, I heard my aunt unleash a high-
pitched squeal, and before I knew it she had me wrapped tightly
in her arms. "Let me look at you," she said. She examined every
inch of me with her wide chestnut eyes. I always forgot how
pretty she was, with her long, silky hair pulled back in a ponytail
and her slender, oval face. Her eyebrows always seemed
perfect—not too full or too thin—and were raised high above
her eyes, adding to the drama of her already expressive
personality.

"My God, Güera, you're taller than me!"

She stood there gawking, with her hands on her slender
hips and her weight shifted to one side. It was true, we were now
virtually the same height, and come to think of it, the same build.
She took hold of my hands and spread my arms out wide. Then
she giggled, let them drop and blurted, "You've grown boobs!"

I'm sure I was beet red as she led me by the hand and
danced her way into the kitchen, where the *cumbia* was now at full
volume. My mom was up on the counter with her legs crossed,
taking in drags from a cigarette and exhaling the smoke out the
window. Still wearing her uniform, Carla sat provocatively on
Shakey's lap at the table, slowly stroking the hand he had placed
on her thigh.

"Hey baby," my mother chirped between puffs, flashing a
relaxed smile that I hadn't seen for quite some time. "How was
school?"

"It was fine," I said, feeling a glare coming from my
sister. "Where's Dad?"

"Softball tournament," answered my mother with a slight
smirk. She exchanged glances with Gina, who broke into a
celebratory twirl in the middle of the kitchen. Now that Carla and
I were older, Gina made no secret of her loathing for our father.

Just as my mom started to ask me what kind of pizza I
wanted, Gina's son Adrian came bursting into the kitchen from
the backyard and flung his arms around my waist. He had grown
since I'd seen him last, but still seemed small for a seven-year-old.
Clutching me with one arm, he looked up with a wide grin and
pointed to the space formerly occupied by his two front teeth.

"I lost them!"

"Well, look at you. Did the tooth fairy leave you money?"

"Uh huh," he said. He shook his head faster and faster until he lost his balance and flopped to the floor. Giggling, he sprawled out and flapped his arms and legs as if making snow angels.

"Get up, you little *loco*," ordered Gina, half-serious. "Before they kick us out."

As I watched Gina mop Adrian's sweaty forehead with a paper towel, I wondered how they were getting along. It was just the two of them, and I knew money was tight. Up until a couple years before, I had never given it a thought that a man had always been absent from their lives. I hate to say this, but being an unwed mother probably had a lot to do with why my father disapproved of Gina so much. But seeing the way she affectionately scooped Adrian into her lap and pelted him with kisses, and witnessing his equally jovial response, I couldn't help thinking that maybe Gina was doing something right, something that my father just couldn't allow himself to admit.

Adrian only sat still in small spurts during dinner, opting instead to see how many times he could run around the kitchen table without getting caught. Gina made a weak attempt to stop him each time he ran past her, but she appeared more interested in the conversation she was having with my mother as they huddled together at the end of the table. Carla and Shakey had already gone back to her room. I could only imagine the naughtiness going on behind the door.

I still didn't understand what she saw in him, but whatever it was, it had kept her going for more than six months. The handful of times I had been around Shakey, he was always draped in black from head to toe and wore the same baggy pants that bunched up around his ankles. Even his limp, stringy hair was black as oil and now that I think about it, probably the result of a bad dye job. He towered over my sister, which I'm sure she liked because it made her feel small in her bodacious body. I guess his height was enough to blind her to the sunken look he had about him, but to me he looked disgusting, as if something had sucked the meat right off his bones. As much as I hated Carla sometimes, I had to admit she was beautiful in a striking sort of way, kind of like Gina, and what she was doing with the likes of Shakey left me wondering why she had set her standards so low.

That afternoon, when I accepted Beth's offer to drive me home, I had really messed up in assuming that June wouldn't be mad. In fact, she was furious and wouldn't speak to me for the entire Labor Day weekend. From what I finally got out of her after days of unreturned calls, she'd had quite a scare when she couldn't find me. Not knowing what to do, she'd driven around the campus and even got out and asked a few "snotty" girls, as she put it, if they had seen me. She finally gave up, she said, and went home trembling, convinced that it would be all her fault for being late if my body turned up floating in some river. I guess that's when she called my house, and my sister answered, casually informing her that I was safe at home after being dropped off by "two dykes in a Jeep."

Oh, not a good move.

I tried explaining to June the reason why I'd gotten into Beth's Jeep that Friday afternoon, but she wouldn't buy it. She accused me of hanging our friendship out to dry now that I was one of "those Saint Agnes girls." So over the weekend, I decided to write her an apology and even rode my bike the four miles to her house to drop it off. She ended up calling me the next day, not mentioning the note I'd left taped to her front door, but I knew it had softened her enough to pick up the phone. The conversation consisted of small talk—mainly gossip about the other students at Pope Pius. And even though she didn't ask me once about how things were going at Saint Agnes, I was just glad we were on speaking terms again and could finally put the whole issue of Friday afternoon behind us.

Not speaking to June all weekend had allowed me ample time to complete the mounds of homework my teachers had dumped on us the previous week. I really could have used her help in geometry, because I was already having problems using the compass. I'd heard that Saint Agnes was all about academics, but I was surprised at the amount of homework so soon— especially over a three-day holiday weekend. As I closed my books Monday evening, I started to get a little panicky at the thought of juggling all my classes, practicing every day and traveling to away games. But before I could work myself into too much of a tizzy, my father let himself into my room and informed me that he'd just gotten off the phone with Coach Krum.

My heart gave a lurch and I sat straight up in my bed, causing some loose papers to fall off the side. I'd told Dad about making the team, of course, but I knew he'd wanted to talk to the coach himself.

"Coach Krum told me you gave a good showing last week, but I finally got it out of him that you still need work on that jump shot."

My father lowered himself next to me onto the bed. I was still trying to process what he was saying. More papers slid to the floor.

"I think I need to work with you more on it. There's just something you're still not getting." He stood up as if angry and started to walk out. I didn't move, worried that I might set him off.

"Oh, and he thinks your glasses are getting in the way, so I'll have your mother take you to the eye doctor for some contact lenses."

I remember him mumbling something else about my jump shot, but I was still in shock about the contacts. I hated my glasses but was resigned to the fact that I'd never be rid of them. I'd always believed that contacts were to be worn by the rich, making them much too expensive for my parents to afford. Never in a million years could I have predicted that my basketball coach would be the one to get them for me, in a roundabout way.

"Are you listening to me?"

My eyes focused again on my father, who was standing impatiently by the door. "Now, Lauren!" His shouting made me jump. "I want you to practice now!"

"Okay, just give me a minute."

My pulse was racing as I rushed out to the driveway, where my father was crouching over on the pavement. As I stooped down to tie my high-tops, taking care to tighten them up the way he always wanted, I glanced at what he was doing. He was bent over making foot-long chalk marks on the concrete, creating a perimeter around the basket.

"You're to start back a ways, take a few dribbles and shoot from the lines. I want you working all the angles."

And so I did, much to his dissatisfaction.

He charged over and ripped the ball from my hands. "No! You release the ball midair—at your highest point—and *not* at the beginning of your jump!" He demonstrated, sinking the shot.

I could feel a wall of tears pressing outward from my eyes. "Okay."

He took an invisible shot, exaggerating the move in slow motion. "It's called a *fade*, Lauren. You fade away so the defender can't block your shot. It's all in the timing. For God's sake, Lauren, we've talked about this!"

My father threw up his hands and turned away as the dam broke and water poured from my eyes. "What the hell is this? Now you're going to cry? Is that your plan for getting out of practicing?"

I tasted a bitter saltiness on my lips and looked at the ground. "No."

He shoved the ball into my stomach, nearly knocking me off balance. "Then do it again and this time, do it right."

But it was no use. My hands were shaking so hard that I couldn't even hold the ball steady. And I couldn't see.

"You're pathetic." My father's voice was a fierce growl. "I don't know why I even waste my time."

He stormed off toward the house and slammed the back door, leaving me there blubbering on the pavement. I sank down to my butt and buried my face between my knees. I didn't understand what I was doing wrong. If he could have just showed me exactly what to do I would have done everything in my power to make it right, to release the ball at the precise moment before my feet landed on the ground. But I just couldn't seem to do it—couldn't seem to figure out how to make my body do what he wanted it to do. It was my fault. If I were a better player, he wouldn't have a reason to be so angry, or to holler and carry on like he always did. Worse, I'd let down Coach Krum and my new team. I just wasn't good enough, and I hated myself for it.

Chapter 9

My father's outburst stayed with me for a few days, leaving me jumpy and on edge. I didn't know who had called whom, but I assumed that if Carl Muchmore was disappointed in me, then Coach Krum probably shared the same sentiments. Plus my mom had yet to schedule me to see the eye doctor, which meant I'd have to endure a few more days of my glasses. So on that first day of official practice, I expected the worst, preparing myself to be cast aside as a second stringer, or worse, as a third.

Somewhere between pulling on my tube socks and lacing up my high-tops, a thunderous chorus of heavy metal music exploded out of the loudspeaker in the locker room. It startled me so much that I nearly fell off the bench. I had the urge to run and hide before someone like Sister Louvois came and started handing out detentions. I think some of the other girls felt the same, because I heard someone say "What the fuck?" That's when a few of the seniors came bounding into the locker room, headbanging the air.

"Pump it up, ladies!"

Beth leaped onto a bench and pretended to air guitar. Some of the other girls jumped up with her, but I just stood there and stared, not feeling at all comfortable with the situation. Practice was about to start, and I didn't want Coach Krum to catch me messing around.

So much for that plan. Before I knew what was happening, Beth had scooped me up by the underarms and was pushing me out into the gymnasium. To my surprise, Coach Krum was standing there in the middle of the court, a grin on his face. "A little loud, don't you think, Polanski? You don't want me to get into trouble with Sister Louvois, now do you?"

Beth dashed past him as he tossed her a ball. "Sorry, Coach, but you said we could pick the song for the first practice." She thundered down court for an easy layup.

"Song's fine, but I also don't want to get shut down on the first day."

Beth rebounded her own ball and then made a sharp pass to Emerson. "Aye, aye, Cap!"

I couldn't believe that Coach Krum was totally in on it. How cool was that? The tension drained out of me and I went to join the other girls for ten warm-up laps around the gym. I hadn't stretched much, so my legs felt tight, but by the time I started working up a sweat, my muscles were fluid and springy. Maybe it was the music that was pumping energy into my veins, but for a few minutes I forgot all about the problem with my jump shot and the fact that I was still wearing my glasses, and actually started to have a little fun.

We didn't scrimmage that day or for many days after that. Instead, Coach Krum worked us like dogs, putting us through series of conditioning drills—some with the ball, some without. He had us constantly on the move, whether passing the ball in figure eight patterns down the court, dribbling between chairs or rebounding off the glass, one after another. On the rare occasion that we'd actually find ourselves at a standstill, it usually meant our thighs were on fire from propping ourselves up against the wall in a seated position. "Endurance is everything," Coach Krum would say as he walked leisurely before us, watching us wince and moan against the wall. "If you're not in pain, then you're not working hard enough."

And work hard I did. At the start of every practice, I always made sure I was the first dressed out and ready to go, and at the end, when Coach Krum made us run suicide drills until we wanted to puke, I was the first to cross the finish line with several seconds to spare. Beth would tell me to slow down and not take things so seriously, but I couldn't allow myself to do that. If I let my effort slip even a little, it could mean the difference between starting and riding the bench.

Plus, my hustle on the court was catching the eye of Coach Krum. He was using me in all sorts of different plays, pitting me against the team's "heavy hitters," who didn't seem so much like threats anymore. I had even managed to break down Emerson, who no longer could stop me from penetrating the paint.

And I have to admit, Coach Krum was right—getting contacts made all the difference in the world. I mean, why don't you try charging the basket through a wall of defenders without your glasses slipping off? Once my dad gave the okay, my mom had me at the eye doctor by the second week of school. If I'd known how much weight Coach Krum's word would carry in my house, I might not have been so reluctant to switch schools in the first place.

So all of that combined, especially the contacts, brewed a newfound air of confidence in me. I was slowly becoming a weapon—I knew it, and my teammates knew it. And by the week of the season opener against the Willowhead Wombats, it was clear that Coach Krum knew it, too.

A couple of things happened that week. The first wasn't a big surprise. After a team vote, Beth was named team captain and Emerson, co-captain. I voted for Beth, because I believed that no one deserved or wanted the post more. Emerson, on the other hand, was more like my *last* choice. But the way it worked, according to Coach Krum, the runner-up traditionally took the co-captain spot as long as he, the head coach, agreed the person deserved it. Knowing the duo was blessed by Coach Krum, I felt obligated to support it and push away any bad feelings I had toward Emerson.

As for the second thing, well, I didn't see it coming. After Coach Krum made the announcement about Beth and Emerson, he dismissed us early, telling us to have a good weekend. As everyone started meandering toward the dressing room, he called to me over the chatter and said that he needed a few words. "Give me about five and meet me in my office," he said stiffly, catching the attention of several of my teammates. Immediately my stomach did a flip. I was nauseated, and my queasiness worsened when a few of the girls began going on in a singsong voice about how "Muchmore's in trouble" and "Muchmore's going to get it." It must have been pretty bad if he wanted to speak to me in his office—alone. My hands started to shake and the only thing I knew to calm myself was to shoot around, but of course I missed every single shot. I was too busy racking my brains trying to figure out what the hell I had done wrong to fall out of favor with Coach Krum.

After five very long minutes, I crept into his office like a miserable little mouse.

"Lauren, come in, come in. Sit down."

As I lowered myself timidly onto one of two foldout chairs in front of his desk, Coach Krum shuffled some papers together and placed them neatly in a pile. A large ornate tapestry of the Saint Agnes crest hung on the wall behind him. Made of a silky material that shimmered in the light, it created a perfect backdrop for a man of his authority.

My eyes wandered his office further, stopping on a gold-rimmed picture frame on the edge of his desk. It held a photograph of an attractive woman and a little girl grinning from ear to ear, both white blond and perfect. They wore matching sundresses and sat in a sea of bluebonnets.

"Beautiful, aren't they?" he said, following my eyes to the frame. Then he leaned back in his chair, which creaked under his weight, and folded his arms behind his head. His eyes burrowed into me, and I quickly found the tops of my shoes. No one had ever looked at me like that before, with such intensity. I felt a prickle of heat dance across my neck and I shifted in my chair. Something had stirred inside me, a certain possibility.

"So," he said. "How are we doing?"

"The team?" I asked. I wasn't sure whether this was a trick question.

"No, no—you!" he said, grinning. "How are *you* doing?"

"Fine," I nodded. My neck seared with heat.

"Just fine? Is Saint Agnes treating you that bad?"

"Oh no, not at all. I mean, it's a great place. Everyone's really nice."

"Are they, now? Well, that's good to know. Sometimes you start to wonder whether there's really something to all the gossip."

"Gossip?"

"You of all people should know, coming to us from Pius."

"I'm not sure I know what you mean?"

"Lauren, I'm sorry," he said, folding his hands in front of him and shaking his head. "You're probably wondering why the hell I asked you to come in here. And really, I just wanted to know how things are going—how *you're* doing."

I felt the tension leave my body as my coach went on to tell me that he understood how hard it must be as the new girl. From what he could see, he said, everyone on the team really liked me. "You even had several votes cast in your favor."

"I did?"

"Yeah, but you know I can't go giving the post to a sophomore. That would get me in loads of trouble. But I can't blame them for wanting you. You've become an incredibly valuable addition. I see you as a future leader for this team."

I couldn't believe it. This whole time I'd assumed he'd brought me into his office just to yell at me about how badly I was doing. Boy, was I relieved.

"Lauren, there is something else I need to talk to you about."

Here it comes, I thought, the part about my jump shot.

"I spoke to your father the other night, but I didn't tell him. I wanted you to be the first to know, as this could be a potentially delicate situation."

He sniffed loudly and folded his arms over his chest. "I'm starting you at point guard and moving Beth to number two."

"What?" I thought for sure I had heard him incorrectly.

"You're the starting point guard. I'm letting Beth know over the weekend."

So many thoughts charged through my mind at once. *Oh my gosh, I'm the point guard . . . he doesn't think I'm a bad player after all . . . how will Beth take this . . . how will the other girls take this . . . why didn't he tell my dad?*

"I wanted to break the news to you separately because I won't lie to you, Beth won't be happy about this. But she's a strong player with a good heart and I know she likes you. Give her time. She'll come around."

I felt like I had just been handed the lead role in the school play. Me, the starting point guard.

"You might get some backlash from some of the other players—particularly the older ones like Emerson. But don't worry about them. Just keep doing what you're doing and I'll handle anything that might flare up. But again, you're already well respected and they know you're a damn good basketball player. No one can deny that."

My neck was on fire.

"Does all that sound good to you?"

Had I really heard him say that I was a good player?

"Uh, Lauren? Ya still with me?"

"Oh yes, I'm sorry. Yes, it's great. Thank you."

"You don't have to thank me, you earned it," he said. "You're one of the hardest working athletes I've ever coached. Do you have any questions?"

"No, I don't think so." I still was in shock about the whole thing, still taken aback by the fact that I had pleased him so much.

"Lauren? Are you okay?"

My eyes snapped back to his. "Yes, yes, I am. But I do have a question."

"Well, by all means, then." His tone gave a hint of impatience.

"What can I do to help my jump shot?"

"Your jump shot?"

"You told my dad that it needed work."

"I did?" He looked perplexed. "Oh, *that*. Well, we all have something to improve on, don't we? But your jump shot," he said, waving a pen in my direction, "is actually pretty good, one of the better ones on the team."

"Then why—"

"Why did I tell him that? For one thing, he wouldn't let me off the phone until I gave him something that you needed to work on. I told him it was only minor adjustments that are needed. Your pure athletic ability will probably help you correct it over time. I wouldn't worry."

"But I need something to take back to my father . . . a drill or exercise that I can do to make it better."

"Like I said, it's nothing to worry about. I'd rather you focus on our first game. Now that'll be a test for sure of what you're made of. Why are you so concerned?"

I hesitated for a moment, unsure of how to go on. In those days, I rarely put into words how difficult life was with my father, and I was convinced that no one would believe me anyway.

"Lauren, it's okay. You can talk to me."

You can talk to me. No adult had ever offered those words, not even my own parents. I had grown accustomed to keeping things to myself—things that were painful and upsetting. But the idea of talking to someone was liberating, at least as far as I'd let it be.

I spoke almost in a whisper, feeling guilty the moment the words left my mouth. "My father wasn't very happy with me after he talked to you."

"I don't understand," he said. "I had nothing but great things to say about your performance so far. I'll give him another call and tell him again how well you're doing."

As he reached for the phone, I panicked, throwing my hands out in front of me. "No, no! Please don't!"

He looked at me quizzically.

"It'll make things worse."

"Okay, okay, I won't call," he said, slowly lowering the phone back to its base.

"Thank you."

He moved his hand over his mouth and rubbed his chin. His face was still clean shaven—a definite improvement from the mustache. His features were smooth and chiseled, except for the pockmarks on his cheeks left over from adolescence.

He flipped his hand to dismiss me. "Well, I guess that's it, then." As he started to stand, he stopped and looked me in the eye. "Unless there's something else you want to discuss?"

"Yes. A drill. I need some kind of drill to do—to show my father I'm serious about getting it right."

Coach Krum eased himself back into his chair. "A drill? I'm not sure there's really a drill to help a jump shot. But there is one thing I can show you."

He pretended to shoot an invisible basketball into an invisible net on the opposite end of the room. I watched as he flicked his wrist in an exaggerated motion, as if tipping the ball into the net.

"It's all in the wrist." He repeated the motion. "Tell him it's all in the wrist. Say that I told you to walk around the house and shoot invisible baskets. Then go out on the driveway with a basketball and do the same thing, but shoot the ball directly upward, catch it and repeat. Shoot, catch and repeat. Pretty soon any shot you take will be one perfect, fluid motion and you'll be guaranteed, with some luck, not to miss."

He bowed his head slightly as if expecting applause. I couldn't help smiling at his enthusiasm—and at his playful manner.

"Thanks, Coach," I said, pleased that I'd have something to take back to my father. "Thanks. Thanks for everything."

"You're very welcome, Lauren. I'm glad you're on the team."

I was almost to the door when he stopped me.

"Lauren, one more thing."

A surge of adrenaline shot through me as I turned around. "Yes?"

He rose from his chair. "The contacts . . . they've made a big difference." He walked out from around his desk and stopped a yard or so away, but he wasn't so far that I couldn't see the vein throbbing on his forehead.

"Your eyes . . . they're nice."

I found my feet again. After a second or two, I glanced up and he locked on me again, this time with an impish grin. But this time I couldn't pull my eyes away. Then I felt his hand rest on my shoulder.

"Well, have a good weekend. You deserve it."

Chapter 10

The moment he touched me, a dizzying surge of energy whipped through me like a lightning bolt. Before he even removed his hand from my shoulder I was through the door, past the weight room and into the gym, in a full-out run.

You've got to understand, I didn't expect to react this way, nor did I know the reason for getting so bothered. All I knew was that one minute we were talking about basketball, and the next, he was complimenting my eyes. That had never happened before, at least not with a guy. I know, I know, Coach Krum shouldn't have been a "guy" to me. He was a teacher and my coach. But when you're fifteen and a handsome person of the opposite sex tells you that your eyes are "nice," don't you think it would cause you to stumble off balance a bit too?

And that's all it did, really; just nudge me. I mean, come on—me, the object of Daniel Krum's affection? Do you not remember me telling you about the photo of his drop-dead gorgeous wife and blue-eyed baby girl? Who the hell was I trying to fool? I chalked it up to a momentary loss of sanity, blaming it on my overly excitable imagination. End of story.

When I finally got to the parking lot, I found June waiting in her car with the engine running.

"I was starting to think you had ditched me again."

I must have shot her a scowl because she immediately recoiled and asked me what was wrong, and then pointed out the red blotches on my neck.

"Hives. Yeah, I know."

"But you only get those when you're really nervous or embarrassed."

Damn it. She was onto me.

"I also get them when I'm really hot. Practice was a killer."

"But why were you so late in coming out?"

"I was talking to the coach."

"For over twenty minutes?"

God, it was virtually impossible to get anything past this girl.

"Who are you, my mother? June, we were talking about basketball stuff, okay? You wouldn't care anyway."

"Well, thanks a lot!" she said, cutting a corner too close and checking the curb. "Why are you in such a bad mood?"

"I'm not. I'm sorry," I said, trying to sound remorseful. "He made me the starting point guard."

"Is that good?"

As you can see, June wasn't too knowledgeable on the whole sports thing, and that was fine with me. I didn't feel like explaining it to her anyway. In fact, I really didn't feel like talking, period, which I think irritated her pretty well since we had planned a sleepover at her house that night. To make our time together even more tense, later in the evening she broke the news to me that we'd be going to Memorial College Preparatory School's homecoming dance with two boys I'd never met.

"But Lauren, I told Jeremy that you could go with his friend Fisher!"

"So you just *now* decided to tell me that you have a boyfriend?" I said, placing my hands on my hips.

"He's not my boyfriend—he's just a friend."

"Since when do you talk to guys?"

"I told you—I went to the Memorial Day football game with Roslyn and met him there. It's no big deal."

"Roslyn Winkler, the sprinkler?"

"Yes, the sprinkler!"

"I thought you hated her?"

"No, I never hated her—she just annoyed me. But that's beside the point. Look, I met Fisher, and he's really nice."

"Oh come off it, June!"

"Really, he's nice and funny, too. I swear. Lauren, puh-leeze?"

After putting up with her whining for an hour, I finally gave in and said I'd go to the stupid dance. I had no desire to meet this Fisher person—with a name like that, the guy had to be weird—but I was willing to do June a favor. And from the way she bounced around her room once I'd agreed to the whole thing, I could tell she was genuinely excited, which I'll admit got me a little interested in the idea of getting all dressed up, too.

"I told him you're a badass player on the Saint Agnes basketball team."

"June, don't go telling him that! What if he thinks you're setting him up with some ugly jock?"

"I thought you didn't care what he thought?"

"I don't. Oh, just never mind."

"I showed him your yearbook picture."

"You did what?"

"Don't worry, I told him you ditched the glasses and are thinner in the face."

"For crying out loud, June, what are you trying to do to me?"

"Hey, at least you get to go to your school's homecoming. You can thank me for that."

June had a point. Since Memorial College Prep was the brother school to Saint Agnes, it was tradition that the two schools did homecoming together. So why not go? I was entitled, wasn't I? I mean, Saint Agnes was my new school now, right? Maybe this would mark a new beginning for me. Perhaps it might even allow me to make some new friends.

As June bounded around her room, trying different hairstyles and pieces of her mother's jewelry, I realized that the two of us needed this. We needed to start acting like high school girls, instead of always lurking around in the background as if we were still in the eighth grade. More importantly, we needed something special again for only us to share.

That night, as I floated next to June in her waterbed, it seemed impossible to find sleep. My mind churned like an engine, producing one thought after another, like an assembly line gone haywire. In the twilight of her room, I reflected on how my life had changed. I was at a new school, and so far the transition hadn't been that bad. I thought about my new contacts and the fact that I'd have to get a new dress for the homecoming dance. I thought about Sister Louvois patrolling the halls at the start of every morning and about Beth being named captain. I thought about Saint Agnes and how young she had been when she died. And then, as June's heavy breathing turned into a rhythmic snore, my thoughts drifted to Daniel Krum and the comment he had made about my eyes. This stayed with me for a while, along with a tickly feeling in my tummy. And then my mind wandered off a little further, to a place of make-believe. Daniel Krum was there, too, and this time his comments went further than just my eyes.

• • •

When I broke the news of my promotion to point guard, my father was standing over his drafting table in the study. At first he acted as if he didn't believe what he was hearing, but once it registered, his forehead immediately softened and an expression of sheer joy spread across his face. He approached me, took hold of my hands and guided me to my knees. He bowed his head and I followed. And then he began to pray in a soft, gentle voice, giving thanks to God for bestowing on us this gift of great fortune . . . thanking Him, our almighty God the Father, for guiding Coach Krum in this most important decision . . . thanking the Lord Jesus Christ for overlooking my shortcomings and for granting me this wonderful opportunity.

At one point he opened his eyes as if signaling to me that it was now my turn. Then he closed them, waiting for me to begin. So I began to pray, carefully choosing words that I knew would please him. "Thank you, Lord," I began, "for blessing me with this honor, for I'm not worthy of it. Thank you, Lord Jesus, for giving me the opportunity to play for such a wonderful team. Please give me the strength to perform to the best of my ability, for all that I do is to glorify you and is impossible without your grace." We continued on like this for several minutes, until I thought his head would burst from clenching his eyes shut so tight. To anyone who wasn't used to seeing this kind of spectacle, it probably looked as if he were bearing down for a rather large and painful movement of his bowels.

After our impromptu prayer service, my father seemed to float through the rest of the weekend in a state of quiet elation. Except for Sundays, family dinners were pretty much nonexistent because of everyone's schedules, so most of the time we'd just fend for ourselves unless told otherwise. That was fine by me. Better to stay apart than risk an argument. But at dinner on that Sunday night, my father was uncharacteristically pleasant, even asking Carla how school was going and speaking almost kindly to my mother.

"Since when do you give a shit about what I do?" sneered Carla with a look of suspicion.

"Can I not ask how my daughter is doing?" said my father through gritted teeth.

"Why don't we try and enjoy our dinner?" said my mother. She took a sip of her water, and I caught a glimpse of her hand. It was shaking.

"Louise, you're right," said my father. "We need to enjoy this dinner because this is a celebration."

"A celebration, Carl? I don't understand?"

"Why, yes! Your daughter has been named the starting point guard for Saint Agnes," he said, looking at me with a broad smile. "I daresay that's a heck of a reason to celebrate!"

"Baby, that's great. Why didn't you tell me?"

"Why didn't I tell you?" I paused, and tried to think of something to say that wouldn't get my mom in trouble. I finally just shrugged, and went off to try not to think too much about my first game as a Lady Lamb.

Chapter 11

I'm not going to spend a lot of time describing to you what it was like to play in a high school basketball game. These events were pretty much the same at any school in America, and still are, so why waste good air recounting what's probably familiar already? The one difference that I will point out was the squad of cheerleaders—fellow Saint Agnes students—who lined up underneath the scoreboard to cheer us on during that first home game. This was an all-girls school, but the thought of girl cheerleaders felt, well, a bit odd. As we ran through our warm-up routine at our end of the court, I couldn't help watching them between shooting drills as they strutted through their chants with sharp precision. They were all very pretty, with their lips brightly painted and their hair drawn up in ribbons and curls, and I watched as they bounced around in tiny brown, yellow and green uniforms that barely covered their behinds. I, on the other hand, was dressed like a sweaty boy in baggy shorts and a sleeveless jersey. The idea of makeup hadn't crossed my mind in quite some time, but looking at those cheerleaders that night, I thought perhaps it should.

I was still trying to shake off the awkward feeling of the cheerleaders when I noticed my father standing at the foot of the bleachers near the entrance, his head craning over the sea of fans making their way slowly to the gymnasium. When we made eye contact, he waved his arms obnoxiously as a clear indication that he wanted me to come over. I looked over at Coach Krum, who was pacing along the bench and thumbing through papers, for permission to go to my father. But when the coach wouldn't look my way, I left my place in the layup line and trotted quickly to my dad.

"What is it, Dad?"

He appeared nervous and unsettled. "Lauren, pray with me."

No, no, no, this is completely unacceptable! I wanted to shout it, but I said nothing as my father took me by the hands and pulled me off to the side. There we knelt hard on the gym floor as people walked by and stared.

Then my father closed his eyes and began to pray out loud—not under his breath, but in full volume so everyone in earshot could hear him give glory to God. I was so angry and so embarrassed that I couldn't breathe. I tried pulling my hands away from his, but he wouldn't let go of my wrists. The more I pulled, the stronger his grip became and the more forceful his prayer resounded. Finally, after we had attracted a fair share of rubberneckers, I felt someone grab me by the shoulders and pull me to my feet.

"The game's about to start."

Coach Krum looked at me with his eyes narrowed. I recognized immediately that he was angry with me, but when he registered that my father was kneeling on the ground too, the situation became clear.

"Mr. Muchmore, Lauren's got a game to play," he said.

As if being addressed by Coach Krum was a direct command from God, my father skulked away like a skittish animal, brushing past the crowd of spectators and disappearing through the door.

I didn't bother to see where he went after that, and I was too angry and humiliated to even care. I had too much to worry about, like getting all the plays straight in my head and leading my team down the court. But it wasn't more than a couple minutes into the game when my father once again made his presence known.

"Lauren, drive to the basket! Take the shot! Get your head in the game!"

It was like he was on a bullhorn. My father's throaty voice cut through the noisy chatter of the crowd, blocking everything else from my mind. I couldn't hear my teammates call to me. I couldn't hear Coach Krum shouting plays from the sidelines. I couldn't hear the cheerleaders. I couldn't even hear myself think. All I could hear was him.

"Lauren, what are you doing out there? Shoot the ball! Damn it! Shoot the ball!"

It happened in a split second. The ball got stripped from my hands and all I could do was watch as a player from the other team scrambled down the court for an easy layup. As I stood there trying to put my nerves back together, Beth came up behind me on her way to throw in the ball. "Relax," she said, squeezing me on the shoulder. "I'm right here. Let's do this together."

As we went through the next few plays, I could still hear my father hollering at me from the bleachers, but his presence didn't affect me nearly as much as it had at the start of the game. I was too elated by the gesture Beth had shown me. As Coach Krum had predicted, the news of my promotion to point guard hadn't sat well with her; except for the times during practice that required us to interact, we hadn't spoken two words to each other all week. I was beginning to worry that things would stay soured between us for the entire season.

I wonder now if my silence came across as pompous, as if I were rubbing it in her face. But truthfully, I was just scared to approach her, scared that she would reject me. Scared of what a conversation could bring—a confrontation, or possibly a fight? I couldn't bear that at home and I definitely didn't want that with someone I hardly knew. So I had remained silent, staying out of her way in the locker room, keeping three or more players between us during drills and avoiding eye contact. I really thought I was doing the right thing that week, giving her the space that she deserved. But now that I look back, perhaps I could have melted the iciness between us if I had just swallowed my fear and pride and made an attempt to talk to her.

Beth obviously was the bigger, more mature person here by the way she stood by me during that first game. Without her support, I would have completely fallen apart, perhaps even forcing Coach Krum to sit me on the bench in exchange for a second-stringer. Instead, we went on to win that first game by a comfortable margin, with me packing away sixteen points and Beth stacking up a healthy thirteen.

In the locker room after the game, it was clear that Coach Krum was pleased with the outcome. He didn't mention anyone by name but told us that we had given a nice showing of teamwork, which would ultimately get us through the tough season ahead. He cautioned us not to get too excited about this win, though, because we still had harder teams ahead of us.

As everyone starting filing out of the locker room, Coach Krum asked me to stay back for a minute. I expected him to chastise me for my sorry performance at the start of the game, but he said something very much the opposite.

"How are we doing?"

He liked to use the word *we* a lot, but by now I had figured out that he was really asking about me.

"We're okay, I guess."

"Tough night out there, eh?"

"The first half, yes. But thanks to Beth—"

"And your talent."

I couldn't help blushing, especially when he smiled at me in response. I remember thinking that he had a nice smile, one that was very inviting and warm. It made his jaw look strong and defined.

"I'm sorry about my dad."

"Don't be sorry. I'm afraid that's something you can't control." He paused, looking like he wanted to say something more. "Are things going to be okay tonight at home?"

A thousand ways to answer this question swirled through my mind. I was tempted to tell him no, that I didn't know how things would be because my father's temper could be so unpredictable. But I decided not to go there, unsure of whether or not he might pick up the phone and tell my father everything I said. It wasn't like my father hit me or anything, though he did belt Carla and me when were little. Still, I wondered if perhaps one day, when his anger finally boiled over the edge, he'd raise a hand to me and beat me black and blue.

I forced myself to smile. "Oh, everything will be just fine. We won, so he'll be in a really good mood."

I walked outside into the chilly fall air to find my father waiting in the car, the engine running. He didn't speak to me until we were about halfway home, when I finally asked him why Mom hadn't come with him to the game.

"She didn't want to."

A minute or two went by before he spoke to me again. "I'm very disappointed in the way you played tonight, Lauren."

This didn't surprise me at all, only the calmness in his tone.

"Yes, I know, I didn't play good," I said. I wanted him to know that I was listening and that I agreed.

"*Well.* You didn't play *well*," he said, turning to look at me. "What do you think was the problem?"

There was no way I could truthfully answer that question. To me, he was the problem, but to tell my father that would have been like telling Adolf Hitler that he had the Jews all wrong.

"My head wasn't in the game." I knew this answer would please him.

"And why not?"

"I'm not concentrating like I should."

We sat through a few more moments of silence before he started up again. "Did Coach Krum speak to you after the game?"

I nodded.

"Well, Lauren, what did he say?" he asked, his tone rising in frustration.

"He said it was a tough game."

"And?"

"And that I needed to work harder."

I could almost feel the tension release from my father's body. I had told him an outright lie, but one that I knew he wanted to hear. If it hadn't been so dark in the car, I could have sworn a look of satisfaction spread across his face. I realized that I was voluntarily putting myself down, but the fight had long gone out of me. There was no changing my father's mind about certain things, and my work ethic was one of them.

"What's the large girl's name, the one with the dark hair?"

"Beth."

"Beth. Now she's a fine player. If I were Coach Krum, I'd make her point guard until your head's on straight."

I was sitting there wondering the same thing. Why was I the point guard, anyway? Didn't Beth want it and deserve it more than I did?

"I'll be surprised if Coach Krum doesn't pull you off the point after that performance."

By the time we got home, my dad had me convinced that I was probably about the worst athlete to have ever played the game of basketball. As the car rolled into the drive, I noticed that the house looked dark, even though it wasn't yet ten o'clock. My father didn't say anything else to me as he let himself out of the car. He disappeared into the house, leaving me on the darkened driveway to gather my bags on my own. Fatigue set in as I dragged my heavy book bag through the front door. I still had two or three hours of homework waiting for me.

After showering, I wanted so badly to crawl into bed, but my stomach and the stack of books in my backpack reminded me otherwise. So I scrounged around in the kitchen for something to eat and headed back to my room. The door to my parents' bedroom was closed, with no sign of light glowing behind it. I gently pressed my ear to the door to see if I could hear anything, but only silence echoed back at me. I guessed she was asleep and didn't want to be disturbed.

Part of me was a little hurt that my mother hadn't come to my game, especially when she had sounded so genuinely interested in making an appearance. But it wasn't the first time she had disappointed me, and for a passing moment I felt drawn to side with my father's insistence that maybe my mom did need to make more of an effort to be involved in my life.

The next morning, I walked into the kitchen to find my mother's lip split open and freshly crusted with blood. She was doing her best to hide her lip from me as she scurried around the kitchen, asking what I wanted for breakfast. Normally I would find something to eat on my own, but on this particular morning, my mother seemed overly anxious to make sure I left for school with a full stomach. Before I knew it, she was stirring pancake batter and scraping scrambled eggs onto my plate. I was about to ask her how badly her lip hurt when my father walked in.

"Well, this certainly is a nice change of pace," he said. He settled down at the breakfast table, unfolding a white paper napkin across his lap.

My mother didn't say anything in response, and if it weren't for the murmur of the talk radio in the background, I could have sworn I heard a vomiting sound. As usual, I kept my eyes on my plate and shoveled the eggs into my mouth as fast as I could. The rollercoaster inside me was building again, and this time I didn't think I'd be able to hang on.

Chapter 12

I didn't get to speak to my mother about her sore lip until a few days later, when my father was away on an overnight business trip. It was a chilly fall evening and my mother had wrapped herself in a blanket outside on the porch swing. From the kitchen, I could see smoke billowing above her. As I opened the back door, the cheerful sound of an accordion met my ears, tempered by the voice of a Tejano singer belting out a tune from the portable radio. I sat down next to my mother on the swing, the weight of my body moving it to and fro.

"I should really stop this nasty habit." She frowned at the cigarette she was holding between her fingers. I hugged my knees to my chest as she drew another breath of smoke, puckering her lips and exhaling with a sigh. The porch light shed a harsh glow on the lines around her eyes and mouth, making her look much older than her thirty-eight years.

"Mom," I said, hoping not to scare her off. "How's your lip?"

She chuckled as if I had just said something completely ridiculous, and then took another long and pronounced drag.

"It's fine, baby. It's getting better."

She didn't look at me when she said this but instead leaned down to turn the radio off, knowing I couldn't understand a word of Spanish. I often wondered if this bothered her any, that my sister and I couldn't speak her language.

"Your father wasn't very merciful this time."

She turned to me, exposing her sore lip. It looked better now that it was scabbed over. My eyes met hers for a moment, but she quickly looked away before I could really determine if they were just watering or glassy from tears.

"What happened?"

We swung for a little while longer, until she had sucked her cigarette down to a butt.

"I need to be smarter about managing my time."

I could tell she spoke these words through gritted teeth. For the first time, she was coming very close to admitting that my father had hit her.

"I want you to know that I was planning on going to your game, I really was, but Tiffany's mom was late picking her up and I couldn't leave when your father wanted me to."

I was back on the rollercoaster, this time with a car full of guilt. As my mind zoomed up and down the tracks, my self-loathing took hold: *My mother is a prisoner to her own husband …if it weren't for my stupid basketball game, he would never have gotten angry…it's my fault that he hit her.*

I am to blame.

Swinging with her on the porch, I knew I needed to say something—something that would communicate how sorry I was that my dad had hit her because of me. But she didn't give me a chance to really say anything of real substance, or maybe I didn't try hard enough, or else I just didn't know how.

"Mom, I'm . . . I'm so sorry."

By the way she tilted her head back and closed her eyes, I could tell that all the pain she was holding in was about to unravel. My next comments came out jumbled, but she spared me the trouble of finding the right words to fit this delicate moment between mother and daughter.

"Baby, it's not your problem. It's been happening for a long time. I've learned to live with it. I just figured that you're finally old enough to hear the truth. There's no reason for me to lie to you and your sister anymore."

"But Mom!"

"Lauren, please. There's nothing you can do—nothing. It is what it is. Just keep yourself out of it, and in a few years you can escape from all this."

Smashing her cigarette in the nearby flowerpot, my mother quickly changed the subject and asked me how things were going at my new school, another first for her. I gave her all the usual bullshit: it was fine, classes were okay and yes, I liked it. She nodded a lot. I guess she was trying to seem interested and engaged in my life the best she knew how.

Knowing that this might be my only chance, I brought up the whole thing about needing a dress for the homecoming dance. My mom was so preoccupied that the idea of me going on a first date slipped by her entirely, but I really wasn't bothered by it. Deep down I knew she had nothing left. I was more concerned about finding a dress anyway, so I was quite relieved when my mother suggested we go to the mall Friday night during my father's doubleheader. I just hoped she would remember.

"Are you coming in?" I said.

"Nah, I like it out here tonight," she said, looking up at the starry sky. "You go on."

As I got up from the swing, my mother grabbed my hand. "Güera, don't mention anything we talked about to your father. It'll just make things worse. Okay?"

"Yeah, Mom. I won't."

Chapter 13

After practice the next day, I found myself sitting on the curb outside the gym and shielding my bare legs from the chill of the night. My sister had forgotten to pick me up again. I thought about calling June for a ride, but I had been doing a lot of that lately, without offering to spend much quality time in return. Then I thought about calling my mom for a ride. I had sensed an unspoken alliance between us lately, an actual kinship. I think she had begun to realize that I was up against the same thing, the same domineering force of a man. My father's dictatorship had spread from her to me now, and even though she didn't have much of a defense against him, I knew she'd help alleviate the pressure on me when she could.

Her last piano lesson ended at six thirty, and if the kid got picked up on time I could be doing my homework by a quarter after seven. I knew this would spoil any dinner plans she had made, but it was a lot easier than calling my father, who would no doubt give my sister a tongue-lashing if he knew she had left me to find a way home on my own.

I was scrounging around in my backpack for a quarter when I heard my name. Coach Krum was walking toward me, carrying a satchel on one shoulder and a workout bag on the other. He had on warm-ups and a jacket.

"Your sister forget you again?"

Embarrassingly for me, it wasn't the first time he had found me sprawled on the curb after practice. He had even offered on one or two occasions to take me home himself, but I had always politely declined, not wanting to impose on him the burden of delivering me home when I knew his own family must be anxiously awaiting his return.

But that night, his offer to give me a ride sounded very attractive—one that would afford the least disruption to the Muchmore household and get me out of the cold faster than waiting for my mom. So I said yes and walked alongside him to his truck, even allowing him to carry my overloaded backpack. He placed the bags in the cab of the truck and then walked around to my side to open my door. As he reached for the door handle, something nudged me from somewhere deep inside.

The heavy door swung open on a rusty metal hinge. The sound echoed through the empty parking lot. "Here," he broke into my thoughts. "Use this to cover your legs." His eyes shifted to my thighs and he tossed his jacket onto my lap. Had he noticed the goose bumps spreading across my skin?

The truck roared to life. "So, where to?"

"I live over by Maple Shade and Crestline."

He looked over at me and smiled. "That's practically on my way home."

"Good, because this is just so embarrassing."

"What? Is it that bad to be seen with me?"

I laughed. "No, no, that's not it. I meant I can't believe what a loser I am that my coach has to drive me home."

"Loser? You think you're a loser just because your sister is irresponsible?" He chuckled and then shook his head. "That's ridiculous. Is that really how you see yourself?"

I pulled on the drawstrings of my sweatshirt and focused on my hands. "I don't know. I guess."

"Then we've got to work on that," he said. "I don't want anybody on my team feeling like a loser. Especially someone as talented and gifted as you."

That familiar prickly sensation erupted across my neck. Thank God the collar of my sweatshirt covered it.

"Hey, do you mind if we stop by at my house first to let my dog out?" Coach Krum looked at me with a boyish grin.

"Sure," I said, a bit more enthusiastically than usual. "I don't need to be home at any particular time."

I don't need to be home at any particular time. I'm not sure why on earth I said this, knowing as I did that my parents would soon clue in to my absence. I tended to say things that I thought would oblige others, especially when people intimidated me the way he did, in a squirrelly, schoolgirl sort of way.

I won't lie; it was a bit awkward when we arrived at his house. We came through the garage, so I got to see what I'm sure a lot of people didn't. Tanner, the family Labrador, was locked in the laundry room and was more than happy to see us. The dog was so excited that he nearly barreled me over and began running circles around us with his rear end close to the ground. My father had never allowed us to have a dog or any kind of pet, for that matter, so I really didn't know how to act around dogs, especially one who was acting like a maniac, jumping and licking all over me.

"He likes you," Coach Krum said, grabbing Tanner by his collar and pulling him off me. "But then again, he likes everyone."

I quickly stepped inside, but froze at the sight (and stench) of dog doo and a puddle of urine in the middle of the floor. "Oh shit," he said, realizing why I had stopped in my tracks. "Um, just step around it if you can, and go make yourself at home while I clean this up."

Feeling uneasy, I sidestepped the mess, straddled the baby gate and found myself in the kitchen, which was pretty well kept except for the dirty dishes on the counter and the crusted pan of dried macaroni on the stove. The kitchen itself was long and narrow, so I walked the length of it, passing the refrigerator littered with colorings and finger paintings. In the dining room, I was met with a large portrait of the Krum family beaming back at me. It must have been taken during the springtime, maybe at the same time Mrs. Krum and Skylar were photographed in the sea of bluebonnets. The three of them were all nestled together in a grassy meadow, Coach Krum leaning on one arm and his wife and daughter lodged securely against him. Once again I was taken by how beautiful Mrs. Krum was, with her white-blond hair resting softly on her shoulders, her perfect smile and her bright blue eyes gleaming with energy. She seemed to fit comfortably in the nook of her husband's body, looking petite and delicate. Their daughter, grinning toothily, sat in her mother's lap.

The family living area offered up another helping of photos. This time I came nose to nose with a wedding shot: "Jessica and Daniel, November 22, 1982." I did the math and realized it would be their anniversary soon. They looked so happy together, the way they leaned in close, cheek to cheek. She had a beauty-pageant smile and a flawless face to match, and a radiance as bright as the sun. She looked like one of the nicest people on earth.

I lingered awhile studying the photos until I spotted the baby grand through the French doors in the next room. It drew me in, like a fish to a shiny lure.

I walked over to it, sat down and moved my fingers over the keys. It wasn't every day that I got the chance to play a baby grand, and a *Steinway* baby grand at that. I could tell that the instrument hadn't received a good tuning in a while, but the faint pitchiness of its sound didn't discourage me from playing my favorite, "Clair de lune." I put my whole body into it, swaying slightly as the crescendo built and pulling back when all that was needed was a whisper. I remember thinking afterward that it was very unlike me to act impulsively like that, to sit down at a strange piano and play my heart out, but something about the moment inspired me. Something about seeing the piano there in Coach Krum's home just begged me to declare *Carpe diem!*

To my surprise, the moment apparently had the same effect on my coach. When that last chord sang out softly from piano's belly, I turned to find him standing in the doorway, leaning to one side with his arm propped over his head and looking at me as if I had just unveiled the secret to immortality. He didn't say anything right away, but instead moved slowly to the armchair next to the window, never taking his eyes off me as he sank into the cushions.

"That was incredible," he said, his expression still one of total amazement. "Where did you learn to play like that?"

"My mother," I answered, feeling my neck prickle with heat.

He dropped his focus on me for a minute while he surveyed the room, looking at it as if for the first time.

"I can't remember the last time I came in here," he said, cocking his head back for a look at the ceiling. "This is a really nice room."

I wasn't sure what to do at that point, if I should get up and apologize for playing his piano or just let him keep talking. My moment of inspiration had long gone, and I was beginning to feel extremely embarrassed for what I had done. But Coach Krum was still relishing his newfound fondness of the room and the fact that I had become the only person to play the piano since he purchased it pre-owned more than four years ago.

"You wouldn't believe what this thing cost me, and it's even pre-owned," he said, motioning to it as if it were a nuisance. "But Jess wanted it for Skylar, saying it was important that she learn to play an instrument since neither of us could. But damn it, did that thing dry me up, a couple months' pay at least, and all because she had to have herself a baby grand."

"Well . . . they're the best," I said, feeling somewhat obligated to defend his wife's lofty taste. "We only have an upright and the sound quality isn't nearly as good."

"So you think we got a good one?"

"Oh yes, it's really nice."

I couldn't help smoothing my hand over the lacquered surface, leaving a shiny trail through the dust. Who knew when it had last received a proper cleaning. What a pity, I thought, to neglect such a superb musical instrument. He had no idea what this piano was truly meant to do, and leaving it idle like this was a waste in every sense of the word.

"So you said your mom taught you to play?"

His question jolted my attention away from the beautiful piano. "Yes, she did. She's a piano teacher."

"Really? Your dad never mentioned that."

"I wouldn't expect him to," I said. But even as they left my mouth, I had already regretted the words and the tone in which they had come. I had never spoken ill of my father and didn't believe it was appropriate—or proper—to start then. If my dad had taught me anything, it was to honor thy father and thy mother. No matter what.

But Coach Krum didn't seem fazed by my comment. He was still stuck on how well I could play the piano. "So, how long have you been playing?"

"Since I was four, I think."

"Have you thought about making a career out of it someday?"

I sat there for a moment, not knowing how to answer him. The suggestion of turning piano into a livelihood caught me off guard. "I haven't really thought about it."

"Well, you should. You're quite good, not that I'm an expert or anything. And if you enjoy it, that's more reason to think more seriously about it."

I certainly couldn't deny that. I did enjoy playing the piano; always had since I could remember. But there was always that one thing holding me back.

"My father really wants me to focus on basketball right now."

I expected Coach Krum to agree with this wholeheartedly, but he came back at me with something quite different. "Is that what you really want to do with your life?"

Again, I didn't answer him right away, but started smoothing my hand over the piano once more. It was the first time someone had asked me what I wanted, the first time someone had taken an interest or cared enough to find out what was going on in my head.

"I don't know," I said, not taking my eyes off the piano. "I just don't know."

"I suppose that's okay," he said, hiking his leg over the chair arm. "I don't think I really knew what I wanted to do either at your age. But I wish now that I had thought more about it than I did. It's nobody's fault; like you, I was really focused on sports. But sometimes I wish someone would have told me to have something to fall back on, for when things didn't work out."

Coach Krum stared up at the ceiling lost in thought. Not used to sitting alone in a room with a man, I pretended to study the piano again until he decided to speak.

"You know, you're really easy to talk to," he said, eyeing me intently as if he was trying to figure me out. "You're like . . . the little sister I never had."

Hearing him label me in this way was disappointing. I wasn't sure, but I didn't want him to see me like a little sister or think of me as a little girl. And suddenly sitting there with him felt very ridiculous, and all I wanted to do was leave.

"Oh my God, it's almost seven thirty," I said, making an exaggerated effort to look at my watch. "My parents are going to kill me."

By the time we were driving through my neighborhood, he had me talking about piano again. I told him about the countless guild competitions I had participated in over the years and how playing in front of a roomful of judges was probably just as bad as being tricked by the Saint Agnes crowd during that ill-fated game the year before.

"You know, the way you handled yourself that night after the crowd totally humiliated you was one of the things that really caught my attention," he said, momentarily taking his eyes off the road. "You didn't let it break you, and that's when I knew I had to have you on my team."

If I'd been drinking something, it would've come out my nose. "Yeah, nerves of steel," I said.

"No, seriously, that took a lot of maturity on your part . . . to keep playing and not let them get to you."

"But they did get to me!"

"Yes, but you didn't let it *show*."

As we pulled up to my house, I was feeling more like his equal again, especially after listening to him go on about how mature he thought I was. The truck had barely come to a stop when I swung the squeaky door open. As I got out, I couldn't help thinking how this might look—my coach dropping me home well after dark. But the idea quickly evaporated from my mind when I realized that I didn't have my key. How the hell was I going to get into the house undetected?

Chapter 14

If my sister was good for anything, it was her knack for sneaking in and out of the house. I can't even begin to tell you the number of times I'd hear her come and go in the middle of the night. She'd lift the window and then clamber through its opening, which I'm sure she had to do carefully to avoid the prickly bushes outside the ledge. Even if I slept through one of her escapes, the next morning the scratches on her arms and legs would always give her away.

On other occasions, I'd awaken to a faint rapping against the screen from the outside. I'd hear the sound of wood scraping against metal, a muffling of two distinct voices and then nothing. I'd lie there in my bed, still as a corpse, straining to hear through the dead calm in the next room. I've got to hand it to them— Carla and Shakey did whatever they did in complete silence. They had to. If my father had ever caught them in the act, he'd most certainly have murdered them both.

But on the night Coach Krum drove me home, I was the one worrying about being murdered if I didn't find an inconspicuous way of entering the house. So I did what Carla would have done; I crawled on my hands and knees across the wet grass in the backyard, lugging my bags right along with me. Light beamed from Carla's window, and I prepared myself for the verbal beating I'd get for trespassing on her territory.

Luckily for me, though, her room appeared empty. I carefully removed the screen and forced the window open. As I pulled myself through the opening, I heard the shower going and knew I had a good chance of reaching my room undetected. Although I hated sharing a bathroom with my sister, I was definitely thankful for it that night.

It was well past midnight when I finally finished my homework and turned out the light, but even then I couldn't stop my mind from racing. It's not like I was worried about anything or upset that nobody in my family had noticed I'd been missing. Sure, I was miffed at first, but every time I started to get worked up about it, I just went back to the time I'd spent with Coach Krum, talking and playing on his Steinway baby grand.

Being with him made me feel safe, made me forget the hell that waited for me at home. From the day he asked my father to leave practice, I had begun seeing him as a force field that nobody could penetrate, question or step around. It was as though I now had someone to step between my father and me, to act as my shield against my father's anger and expectations and his sick fascination to regain through my life what he had lost. I pictured over and over the way Daniel Krum had tracked my lips as I spoke, and the sensation of his eyes burning through me at the piano. Whatever was with him that evening, it left me tossing and turning in my bed, wondering if he was thinking of me at the exact same moment I was thinking of him.

My restlessness worsened with the dawn. I went from a feeling of safety to a deep shade of shame, one so strong that I could hardly bear to look at my reflection in the mirror. By the time I was showered and dressed, I had convinced myself that my preoccupation with Daniel Krum was simply a by-product of wanting attention, and that's what good coaches and teachers did—gave students the attention they deserved. That would be the end, I told myself, of these silly, unwarranted thoughts and misplaced feelings.

At breakfast, Carla pounced on me the moment she slithered into her chair at the table. She was good like that, always knowing when to play me for the fool in front of our dad.

"So where'd ya get the scrapes on your arms?" She leaned over to catch a glimpse of my legs. Our father, who was sitting next to her, craned his head to see what she was looking at.

"At practice I got tangled up with another player scrambling for a loose ball."

Our dad eyed me and kept eating. Still Carla kept staring at me. She was looking for a way to rat me out.

But that morning I was more concerned with catching my mother's attention than with fretting over Carla. My father had his doubleheader that night and I wanted to make sure my mother still intended to take me shopping. Catching her attention, though, was like trying to swat a fly as she darted around the kitchen and fussed over my father's softball uniform.

"It's still a little damp," she said, handing it to him.

"I guess it'll have to do then, won't it." He grabbed it from her and spread it out on the counter. "This could have been avoided if it had gotten done last night."

And just like that, the tension in the room escalated. Without acknowledging the comment, my mother walked over to the sink and began scrubbing dishes.

Please Lord, I begged, don't let there be a fight.

But my father kept sticking around and pawing through his softball bag. It was unlike him to dally like that. I figured there must be something else on his mind.

"It sure would be nice if my family came to watch me play sometimes."

I heard Carla grunt as she slinked off from the table. At the sink, my mother stopped her scrubbing and shut off the faucet, but she didn't turn around to face him.

"I have a makeup lesson tonight," she said in a half-friendly tone. "Maybe another time, Carl."

I felt my stomach drop as the water came back on. I knew he was going to ask me and ruin my only chance of getting a dress for the dance without him finding out.

"Got practice tonight, Dad. Don't know how long it'll go."

"Well, of course you do. I don't want to get in the way of that," he said, glaring at my mother.

About that time, I heard the horn honk, signaling that June was outside waiting. I grabbed my bags and headed for the door, and as I opened it, I felt a light touch on my arm. It was my mom, and she spoke barely above a whisper.

"I canceled my lessons tonight so I could pick you up after practice. What time will you be done?"

"We get done early on Fridays. Five o'clock."

"Okay, baby, I'll be there."

If I had any concerns that my mom wouldn't show, I had plenty of time to think about it. After school, I made my way into the gym and was met by a handful of players laughing and carrying on. The lights were off, and before my eyes had a chance to adjust, several girls hurriedly brushed past me on their way out the door.

"Coach is giving us a freebie tonight," Beth said as she walked toward me with her hand raised for a high five. I raised mine in response, only to have my hand practically whacked off. We hadn't been the same since Coach Krum named me point guard, and I carried a lot of guilt from that. I could tell Beth was still angry from the way she would thrust the ball back to me just a little too hard or elbow me during scrimmages. I guess I figured I deserved it for taking her position, and hoped her coolness toward me eventually would pass.

But as I dawdled that afternoon in the locker room, trying to kill time until five, the loneliness of my situation swept over me. I had no real friends at Saint Agnes, or at least none I really felt I could mesh with. At the beginning of all this, a friendship with Beth had looked promising, but my elevation to point guard had squashed any real hopes of that. As strange as it might sound, Coach Krum was the only one who really seemed to take a genuine interest in me. Nobody else at Saint Agnes knew I played the piano or ever asked how I was doing. Not seeing him that afternoon—especially after going over to his house—made me feel lonelier than I'd been in a long time.

My mood brightened when I finally saw my mom's station wagon wind down the driveway into the parking lot. She showed up like she had promised, and even a few minutes early. It had been a long time since I had gone anywhere with my mother alone. I was looking forward to spending some quality time with her outside of the normal pressure cooker of our family.

But right away I could tell that her mind was miles away from making this into any memorable mother-daughter outing. As we putted along, she hung her head halfway out the window, sucking methodically on her cigarette. She had that same deflated look about her as she had the night I had found her alone on the porch swing. It was like a cloud was resting over her, casting her in such a thick fog that I wondered if she ever would find her way out.

She found her way soon enough when we arrived at the Parkside Mall. As we made our way into Sanger Harris, my mom was the first to spot Aunt Gina and Adrian waving us down in the women's department. Adrian hit me like a bowling ball in the stomach, not with his fist but with such a ferocious hug that he nearly knocked me off balance. Gina ran up in three-inch heels, planted a wet kiss on my cheek and started going on and on about my first homecoming dance. Then Adrian grabbed my hand and started swinging from my arm with a roar of laughter. Before I could tell him that we didn't have time to play, my mom and Gina had already walked ahead of us, arm in arm.

This was not how I had imagined shopping for a dress would be. I had wanted so badly for it to be just the two of us, mother and daughter sauntering along, casually pulling a dress from the rack and holding it up to the light, together deciding that it didn't hit the mark and moving on to the next. And then, after trying on a handful of styles in a fit of laughter, we'd find the one that we both agreed made me almost pretty. Then maybe, if there was time, we'd make our way to the food court for a quick bite, topping the evening with a soft-serve ice cream cone.

But no. It had to be chaotic. It had to be loud. And it had to be a group outing. I knew now why my mom had been so intent on keeping our date: it was a chance for her to see Gina outside my father's radar. Spending time with me had no real appeal for her. That was clear by the way I became virtually invisible the moment she spotted Gina. She was using me, and in a way, Gina was using me too. With me there they were free to carry on together uninterrupted while I played babysitter to

Adrian, who had nothing better to do than swing on the clothes racks like they were monkey bars on a playground.

Still, I was glad that I had remembered to take the wad of cash I had hidden in my music box with me to school that morning. I say it was a wad of cash, but really it was only $42.86, money left over from the lessons I had taught over the summer. After mulling it over in my head, I had concluded that a dress for the homecoming dance was probably the best thing I could spend it on. Plus, I hadn't wanted to make my mom fork out any more money than she had to from her measly piano teacher earnings.

As I had expected, the prices eventually forced us to comb through the sales rack, which offered mostly bigger sizes in the 12 to 14 range. My height and "hour-glass shape" as Gina put it, made it difficult for me to find a good fit. I was hoping to make work a size 6 navy dress with nice lacework on the bodice, but once I pulled it on, Gina was quick to point out that it made me look like a grandmother.

I was about to throw up my hands in despair (and beat Adrian for peeping at me from under the dressing room next to mine) when I heard Gina's trademark squeal. She flung open the dressing room door and declared that she had found the perfect dress. It didn't look like much draped on the hanger, but the color was nice—a deep, rich cranberry that shimmered even in the stale light of the changing area. I immediately protested when I saw the size, but she urged me to try it on anyway, and I finally agreed just to get her off my back.

I was right—it was way too big—but through the frumpiness, I could tell it had potential. The neckline rested off the shoulder but wasn't indecent; and if it had been about three sizes smaller, it would have hit me right above the knee.

"Oh Güera, the color."

I saw it too—the way it brought me to life. It lay against me like a satin bedsheet, enriching the creamy tone in my skin.

"But it's the wrong size."

"But Güera, picture this."

My aunt floated behind me and pinched the fabric on either side of my waist. "Look at what we could do." She rested her chin on my shoulder and looked at my reflection dreamily in the mirror.

"Do you think you could do it in time?" said my mother, who was now standing in the doorway, obviously taken by the same image in the mirror.

"Of course I can, Louisa," Gina said, talking at my reflection. "I can do anything with a dress."

With one hand, she gathered the fabric at the small of my back and with the other, gently shook my hair out of its ponytail holder, combing through it with her fingers until it was smooth. Her chin came back on my shoulder as she let go a heavy sigh.

"See, Louisa, we can make her beautiful."

Chapter 15

I had this sinking feeling in my gut that the whole dress thing would end in disaster. Only a week remained until the dance, and in that time, Gina had promised to tailor the dress to fit me, without me even trying it on midway through its transformation. I was no seamstress, but to take a dress from a size 12 to a 6 was no small feat, and frankly I didn't have much faith that my Aunt Gina, the woman who was always a half step behind on everything, could pull it off.

The plan was for Gina to bring the dress to June's house by four o'clock on Saturday so I could get ready there. Since she was a stylist, my aunt had also offered to do our hair, an idea that June and her mother thought divine. But the idea of Gina coming over to June's house and mixing with the Huis made me feel ill.

Now, as I hear myself admit that to you, I realize I had more of my father in me back then than I'd thought. Or maybe I just wasn't mature enough yet to see past Aunt Gina's flaws to the wonderful person inside. Because to my surprise, Gina showed up at June's house that afternoon ten minutes early with dress in hand and a cosmetic case full of makeup and styling tools—all this and *without* Adrian. At least it gave me some comfort, knowing that my hellion cousin wouldn't be running amok in the Huis' house.

Still, the minute Mrs. Hui handed Gina a glass of red wine, I wanted to disappear again. Back then, Gina liked her wine and anyone who offered her a glass. You could always tell she'd had too much to drink when she got on her bullhorn. But that night, thank God, she controlled herself with the wine, at least while June and I were still there, and the dress . . . well, she had done a fine job with it. When I came out with my dress on, June, Mrs. Hui and Gina just stared at me with their bottom lips hanging open. I was afraid at first that they found it repulsive, but it wasn't long before they broke into a tremendous chorus, going on and on about how beautiful I looked. And I did feel beautiful, and a lot older standing there in heels and in a dress that hugged every part of my body. Gina assured me that the curves it gave me were in good taste, though I felt awkward and bashful, almost as if I were doing something wrong.

That's about the time that Mrs. Hui offered me some wine, telling me that it would help calm my nerves. She let June have some too, and it wasn't long before we were giggling. I felt like I was floating, as if I were outside of myself looking in. That glass of wine tripped something inside me, or maybe woke the part of me that didn't give a shit. It dulled the side of me that didn't know how to relax, the side of me that was always ready to bound away before the shouting started and the angry words were thrown.

I really wasn't surprised that Mrs. Hui let us have wine. It certainly wasn't June's first time. June told me it was a European thing, a French custom for older children to drink wine alongside their parents at special occasions. I didn't really know if this was right or wrong, but one thing was certain: my father would have considered it a terrible disgrace. I wasn't about to let him find out.

Of course, I couldn't let him find out about any of this. Now that June and I went to different schools, the chance of our parents running into each other had diminished greatly. But I was deathly afraid that June's mom or dad would let it slip if they met him at the store or at another random location. Even letting my sister find out could potentially be harmful; she'd run her mouth to our father just to get me in trouble. But in the end it wasn't me that I was worried about. Sure, my father would probably ground me for a year, but my mom would suffer the worst at his hands. I had dreams about it, him killing her. And every time she'd die, I'd always end up the one responsible for sparking his rage.

The wine helped me temporarily erase this vision from my mind. And once Gina started fussing with my hair, my worries diffused into distant thoughts. She had just finished putting June's hair in an updo with a cascade of curls spilling down the side. June and her mother loved it, and I'll admit it looked great on her, but I wasn't really into a lot of curls and hairspray. The dress I had on was bound to draw attention enough.

Gina had good instincts when it came to hair, because after she tried out a number of different upswept styles on me, she finally let my hair fall naturally to my shoulders.

I patted down a few flyaway strands. "See, it never wants to do anything. It's just so thin and blah."

Gina slapped me playfully on the wrist with the comb. "I'm not finished! Have some patience, girl."

So I sat there while she teased and sprayed, smoothed and combed. And when finally she was done, I saw a strange girl staring back at me, a girl who was almost beautiful. My characteristically drab and mousy hair had volume and shine with a hint of soft curl. Gina studied my reflection in the mirror. "It still needs something more," she said, bending down to rummage through her bag. Out of it she pulled a wide black silk ribbon, and before I knew what was happening, she had positioned it like a headband, tying it at the base of my neck and hiding the knot under my hair.

"There. Now it's perfect." She smoothed my bangs to the side and gently tucked them under the ribbon, securing them with a bobby pin.

June stood in the doorway, gawking at me. "I almost don't recognize you. Seriously, Lauren, you look really pretty."

Gina reached into her bag and pulled out a black velvet box. "Wait, I've got one more thing." She opened it and took out two pearl earrings and a single pearl drop on a thin silver chain. "Wear these tonight," she said, securing a pearl to my ear. "These were your grandmother's."

I touched my lobe, overcome by the smooth, white ball. "They're beautiful."

Gina wrapped her arms around my neck and rested her chin on my shoulder. "She'd be so proud that you're wearing them." My aunt's voice broke slightly. Then she started busying herself putting things away in her bag.

The moment did not move me as it did her. I never really got to know my grandmother, and I blame my father for that. His dislike of my mom's family ruined any real chance of a relationship. But my few memories of my grandmother are warm and gentle. She loved to take me into her lap and wrap me in her arms, and then whisper in my ear. *Bonita, bonita. Te amo.* Maybe Gina wanted to remind me of that, or else she was trying to make an effort to reach me, to really connect with me on a level that in a normal family, a loving one, would come as easy as a hug.

•••

My date that night, Fisher Linardakis, turned out to be incredibly annoying. I don't think I'd ever met anyone so hyper in all my life. His lips moved faster than he could get his words out, so I gave up early on trying to keep up. On the ride to the dance, a U2 song came on and I thought he might burst. He pulled out a pair of drumsticks from his sport coat and drummed the inside of the car for the entire song. Then he went on a rant about playing the drums as well as someone named Larry Mullen, and when I asked him who that was, he scoffed at me.

"You don't know who Larry Mullen is? Oh my God, he's only one of the best drummers in the world, for the best band in the world!"

"Let me guess, U2?"

"You got it, babe. I'm liking you already."

By the time we arrived at the dance, Fisher had beads of sweat running down his temples from all his manic drumming, and I, a growing urge to call it a night. I didn't know what was more nauseating, the wine I had drunk or the way Fisher kept winking at me. I tried getting June's attention as the four of us made our way into the auditorium, but there was no getting through to her. I could tell that her so-called friend was quickly becoming more than just that, and I figured that for her sake I could stick it out with this Fish person for at least a couple more hours, as long as he behaved himself somewhat.

However, after only a few minutes of listening to Fisher go on about the uncle who he claimed was a famous actor in New York, I decided I needed a break and headed for the bathroom. And that's when I spotted Coach Krum, standing off to the side with some other teachers near the refreshment table. Suddenly embarrassed, I hurried blindly toward the bathrooms, nearly colliding with a group of upperclassmen from Saint Agnes. By the time I was finally safe behind a stall, I had lost all need to urinate and instead took advantage of the privacy to collect myself and think about why in God's name I was feeling so crazed.

But I couldn't put my finger on it, and I knew that I couldn't stay there all night. So I left the toilet and checked myself over in the mirror. Something wasn't right. I washed my hands—twice—and looked again. And then I saw it: a little girl. Without even thinking, I tore off the black headband and stuffed it into my purse. I flipped my head over, shook out my roots and whipped my hair back on my shoulders. Body, volume and glamour. No more little girl.

Feeling a couple years older, I ventured back out to the auditorium, where "Just Like Heaven" by The Cure was pouring out of the speakers. Kids flooded the dance floor. I tried not to let my eyes stray over to the refreshment table, but I couldn't help noticing that Coach Krum was no longer there. I craned my head over the bobbing crowd and then stopped on a tall and masculine figure near the underside of the bleachers. I smiled and walked over.

"Coach Krum?"

At first he couldn't place me. Then he fumbled his words. "Oh . . . uh, hi, . . . um."

"Lauren."

"Yes, Lauren. I, uh, almost didn't recognize you."

I felt my neck break out in a million splotches. "Yeah, I know," I said, touching my hair. "This is all my aunt's fault."

"Well, she did an excellent job . . . you're stunning!"

That's about the time my eyes dropped to my shoes and I started to perspire. We stood there talking for I don't know how long while he rocked back and forth on his toes and I twirled my hair.

"So why aren't you out there dancing with your date?"

I rolled my eyes.

"That bad, huh?"

"See for yourself. He's the one over by the loudspeaker, drumming the air."

Coach Krum looked over and cringed. "Ooh. I'm afraid you're right. I guess you'll just have to keep standing here and talking to me then," he said, flashing a grin. "Hope an old guy like me won't bore you too much."

"You're not that old," I said playfully.

"Compared to you, I'm ancient."

"Well, you don't look ancient."

"How old do you think I look?"

"I don't know," I said, twirling my hair again.

"No, come on, tell me," he said, nudging my arm. "How old do you think I am?"

"I already know how old you are. Thirty-five."

"Okay, but how old do you think I *look*?"

I drilled the toe of my shoe on the ground. "I don't know. I guess a lot younger than that."

A rolling laugh escaped from his mouth. "Fair enough. And for what it's worth, you definitely don't look your age tonight, either."

That familiar prickly sensation began spreading across my neck once more. I forced a cough, even though there was no tickle in my throat. Coach Krum offered to get me some punch, and a moment later he returned with a full beverage glass and napkin. I sucked it down, not out of thirst but out of pure fear of letting the conversation go any further. While I drank, I noticed him out of the corner of my eye studying me, his eyes slowly moving up the bodice of my dress.

Then he spoke. "Would you be interested in giving my daughter piano lessons?"

Chapter 16

I always used to think that my first kiss would be the one kiss I'd never forget—the one that would sweep me off my feet and leave me a changed person forever. For a short period of time in the eighth grade, I was convinced that this long-awaited kiss was not far away, and in fact would be delivered by the most popular boy in school—Rex Ryan. Just his name alone would make my heart jump, and when he asked for my number and started calling me, I turned into a lovesick puppy who didn't know better. I remember June saying that the whole thing smelled fishy. Why, she demanded, had the handsomest and coolest guy in our grade suddenly dropped his cheerleader girlfriend (who was blond and beautiful) to start going out with a nobody like me? I told her she was wrong, and that Rex really did like me, and that maybe she should stop this jealousy and just be happy for me. After all, he had called me almost every night for two weeks; that was proof enough that he was into me.

Oh, but don't forget that kids can be mean; they can be very mean. Unfortunately I learned this the hard way, despite June's repeated attempts to bring me back to reality before I got hurt. I was too stubborn to listen to her, too stubborn to consider that maybe, just maybe, this was all part of some elaborate joke. In the end, it was a joke and a painful lesson, especially when it all came out that during my phone conversations with Rex, the ones where he'd tell me how much he liked me, his beautiful cheerleader girlfriend was listening on three-way and quietly tape-recording the whole charade.

But the way I found out was probably worse than the whole trick itself. Rex invited June and me to his house for his birthday party. At the precise moment that we made our way into his parents' living room, his girlfriend, surrounded by all of her cheerleader friends, cued the tape and replayed my phone conversations with Rex, every word for horrible word. Although I didn't stick around to hear even thirty seconds of it, I was told the tape provided most of the entertainment for the evening.

So when I found myself sitting in the back of a car with Fisher after the homecoming dance, I decided to just get the whole first kiss thing over with since obviously it wasn't ever going to happen for me like I had once dreamed. But when I began drowning in the orifice of his mouth, I immediately regretted giving in to him. I started wishing he would just go away, and when he tried placing his hand on my chest, I decided enough was enough and shoved him off me. When I was forced to stiff-arm him, I demanded that Jeremy and June stop sucking face long enough for Jeremy to drive us home.

That night, while June interrogated me about why I didn't like Fisher, my mind wandered back under the bleachers. When she finally fell asleep, I was glad to be rid of her pestering, but more than anything, I was finally free to begin plotting a way to convince my dad that giving piano lessons to Skylar Krum was a good idea. Coach Krum still needed to discuss the whole thing with his wife, so I figured I needed to secure an answer quickly from my father just in case it turned out to be a no.

I had a mixed-up bag of reasons for wanting to do it. For one thing, I didn't want to disappoint Coach Krum, not after seeing how excited he'd gotten about the possibility of me teaching his daughter the piano. And I could get my hands back on that baby grand. Beyond that, beyond even the thrill of playing such a fine instrument, I had too many emotions swarming around me to really make sense of any of them. The more I tried swatting them away, the stronger they became. And standing there under the bleachers that night with Coach Krum didn't help any. We'd worked out almost all of the details. I'd come over Saturday afternoons for about an hour. This way, the lessons wouldn't interfere with basketball practice or my homework time, and since Skylar had finally dropped her afternoon nap, it was easier, he said, to schedule activities for her. We'd even negotiated a rate—ten dollars for each lesson. To a teenager in 1989, that was pretty darn good.

I didn't waste any time speaking to my father about the lessons, although I did make sure my plan for approaching him was straight in my mind first. I waited until Sunday afternoon, when I knew he'd be working in his study. I appeared in the doorway with a basketball tucked under my arm and invited him out to the driveway, where I promised to show him an improved jump shot.

"Well, it's about time," he said, pulling on his coat.

Thankfully, I was right on with my technique that day. I could tell my dad was impressed with my jump shot by the way he nodded approvingly and clapped when the ball slid through the net. I made it a point to mention that Coach Krum had made a special effort to work with me on it, and that if it weren't for his guidance, who knew where my game would be?

"You're right, Lauren, we have a lot to thank him for. I want you to think about how you can show your appreciation, because he could be your ticket to a scholarship if you play your cards right."

I nodded. "I already know of one thing I can do."

"And what's that?"

I spun the basketball on the tip of my finger and then caught it before it dropped. "He asked me to teach his daughter to play the piano."

Just the word itself probably made my father cringe. I'm convinced he loathed everything that had anything to do with the instrument, most likely because he associated it with my mother. He had never supported my interest or talent for the piano; in fact, he always tried to divert any opportunity that would connect me to it further. But the situation I'd laid before him was unique, mainly because it involved the man who he thought hung the moon.

"Did your mother have anything to do with this?"

"No. She knows nothing about it. Coach Krum mentioned that his wife wanted his daughter to learn the piano, and I told him I used to play."

"I see. And this would be something that would please him?"

"Yes, very much so," I said, making myself smile. "But I believe it would please his wife the most."

He flipped his hand in the air and shook his head. "Of course, his wife. I don't think Daniel Krum would be too interested in something like that. But if he sees some sort of importance in it, then it would be good to help him."

"So I can do it?"

My father placed his hand on his chin and rubbed his beard. "As long as it doesn't interfere with your basketball or your schoolwork."

I immediately felt my posture straighten. "It won't. It would just be for an hour on Saturdays."

"So you've already discussed this with him?"

"Oh no," I said quickly, hoping I was being convincing enough. "I wanted to get your permission first, but I thought Saturdays would be best—after the morning practice."

"Well, you need to make sure it works for the Krums' schedule and not just your own."

I nodded faster. "Yes, Dad, I'll make sure."

After I shot around a few more times, my father said he had more work to do. But before he returned to the house, he left me with a parting comment.

"Just because I'm letting you teach this child a few lessons, I don't want you or your mother to go thinking that this will turn into a habit," he said, pointing at me. "There is nothing for you in piano, and we wouldn't even be discussing this if it didn't have something to do with Daniel Krum. Do you understand me?"

I looked him in the eye and made my voice firm. "Yes, Dad. I hear you loud and clear."

His weight shifted to his heels and he folded his arms. "Good. Because after this is over, your life will be nothing but basketball. Period."

Chapter 17

The next day at school, I could hardly wait to tell Coach Krum that my dad had cleared me to give Skylar lessons. So instead of waiting until after practice, I decided to try to catch him in his classroom during my free period midmorning. When I got down to the science department in the basement and found the room empty, I impatiently tore a sheet of paper from my notebook and started scribbling him a note—a note that I wrote over nearly five times before I finally folded it and nervously placed it on his chair.

Dear Coach Krum,

Good news. My dad said it was okay for me to teach Skylar the piano. I can start this Saturday. I hope you still want me to do it. If you want to talk about it, you can call me on my own line, 349-7835.

Lauren Muchmore

By the time fifth period came around, I was feeling like a complete idiot for having left the note. I mean, notes were for little girls, and I was afraid I had just shown him how immature I still was. And to leave my phone number for a teacher? For crying out loud! I might as well have folded it all silly and drawn smiley faces all over it. Disgusted with myself, I slammed my locker and nearly knocked over several girls on my way to the gym. I had made an ass of myself, and now I'd have to face him for two long hours during practice.

To add to my paranoia, he never even mentioned the note throughout our practice, which made me question if he'd even found the note at all. That turned into yet another self-made nightmare: what if one of his chemistry students had picked it up and was now sharing it with all her friends? And then those girls would spread it around, and I wouldn't be able walk down the hall without someone pointing and snickering at me.

I attempted to shove these worries out of my head as I fought for sleep that night, but as soon as I started to doze, the phone rang loudly on my desk. I jumped out of bed and scampered over to it, my heart firing like a machine gun. Before I could grab it, though, Carla had snatched it up, putting to rest any hope of it being for me.

Just as I had crawled back into bed, Carla swung open the door of our connecting bathroom and barked that some guy was on the line for me.

I shoved my glasses back on my face. "What? Who is it?"

"I don't know, some guy. Don't talk long. Shakey's supposed to call."

Fumbling spastically for the phone, I forgot all about holding the cord steady at the base. When I answered, all I could hear was static.

"Coach Krum?"

"Who's Coach Krum?" It was a squeaky male voice only a year or two shy of puberty.

"Who's *this*?"

"It's the Fish, babe. Who was that who answered the phone? She sounded fine."

God, I wanted to die. I had been certain that it was Coach Krum who was calling. Not in a million years had I expected it to be Fisher.

"How did you get my number?"

I made a mental note to remind June to never give my number out without asking me first. But Fisher having my number in his possession was the least of my worries. I still hadn't heard from Coach Krum, which was making me feel increasingly insecure about the whole situation. I started to think that perhaps I had interpreted his interest in the lessons all wrong and that the enthusiasm he'd shown about the idea was merely a figment of my teenage imagination.

The school week came and went, bringing me finally to Saturday morning practice. Coach had gone easy on us, probably because we'd pulled off our third consecutive win on Thursday. I think we could all feel ourselves settling into a groove, one that I'm sure Coach Krum hoped would take us through the rest of the season unscathed. The one loss that we had suffered so far was a silly one, and if it hadn't been for me and Emerson fouling out, we probably could have held the other team to thirty points or so. I felt pretty responsible for the loss as I did with most things in my life, but Coach Krum didn't seem to be too upset about it. He told us to chalk it up to a learning experience, and thank God we'd identified the potential problem early in the season.

It wasn't until the end of practice that Saturday morning that I finally got a response to my note. Coach Krum leaned down next to me as I hung over my knees to catch my breath after a long set of suicide drills. He thanked me for the note and said that he and Jessica would very much like for me to give lessons to Skylar, and I should come over at one o'clock that day. It wasn't a question but more of a request, so without hesitation I told him I'd be there, even though I wasn't remotely close to being prepared.

When my dad picked me up from practice, my voice dropped out of me. He had that faraway look again, the one that said all his battery power was dangerously low. He hadn't shaved yet either, another sign that the cloud of depression had descended on him. So I didn't want to push him too far by asking him for a ride to the Krums', because I knew that when we got home, my father would walk straight into the house and go to sleep.

When I didn't see my mom's car in the driveway, the time bomb in my gut went off. As soon as I heard my dad close the bedroom door, I dashed into the piano room and started digging through a stack of my mom's sight-reading books and other beginner materials. I was so unprepared, so out of my element. Without my mom to guide me, I was a fish flopping around on the dock, my gills sucking in water that didn't exist.

But I grabbed a couple books of nursery rhymes, hoping they'd suffice, and called June. Thankfully I reached her on the first try. She dropped everything and came right over, along with a million questions as to why I was all of a sudden giving piano lessons to my coach's daughter.

"Why do you think it's so weird?"

"I don't know. He's like a teacher, and since when do students get involved with a teacher's family?"

"Get involved? I'm just giving her lessons. I'm not moving in with them or anything. They're going to pay me, June."

"The extra money will be nice."

"Yeah, ten bucks a lesson."

"You'll be rich!"

"Well, I don't know about that. I'll probably give it to my mom."

"Why do that?"

I knew June didn't understand my reasoning, and I wasn't about to explain it to her. Money in her family wasn't an issue, but in mine it hovered like a black cloud. My dad scrutinized every penny my mom spent, even if she went over by a few bucks at the grocery store. It didn't matter how responsibly she managed the family budget, my father would still find a way to exert his control. Somewhere along the way I'd started to feel partially responsible, perhaps hoping that if I could ease the financial pressures even just a little, maybe my dad would ease up on my mom.

It was in this spirit that I approached the Krum house that day: I was doing this for the extra money and that was all. Coach Krum greeted me at the door with a warm smile, saying that they were glad to have me and that Skylar and her mother were already waiting in the living room. He offered me a soda, which I declined, not wanting to seem too comfortable in a house I'd been in before.

As I followed him, a strong floral scent floated through the air and grew stronger as we approached the living room.

There on the piano bench sat Jessica Krum and little Skylar, who was already fingering the keys. Jessica stood up at the sight of me and prompted Skylar to do the same.

"Hello, Lauren, I'm Jessica Krum," she said rather formally. "This is our daughter, Skylar."

Almost as if she were a windup doll, Skylar offered her hand, which I leaned down to shake. Her baby-fine hair was blond and curly, just like in the photos. She grinned at me, revealing a missing front tooth, and pushed a pair of wire-framed glasses up the bridge of her nose.

"She just got glasses last week, so we're still trying to get used to them," said Coach Krum, ruffling his daughter's hair.

"But the eye doctor says she won't have to wear them long," Mrs. Krum said quickly. "We're hoping that means we can take them off by next year."

Although this meant nothing to me, I nodded and smiled anyway, still nervous about being there to begin with. From the way they stood glued to the side of their daughter, I assumed that Coach Krum and his wife would stay in the room during the lesson. This appeared to be the intention of Mrs. Krum, who sank into the oversize chair opposite the piano. But before she could get comfortable, Coach Krum leaned down and whispered into her ear, then eased her up by the hand and guided her out of the room. I felt a rush of relief as I watched them leave, knowing that I could proceed with the girl in private.

Since my only other piano student had been something of a menace, I came prepared to deal with temper tantrums, defiance and downright bratty behavior. With the Krum girl, though, my experience turned out to be completely different, and in fact completely enjoyable. So much so that by the time I had her playing "March of the Pony" at the end of our first lesson, I thought perhaps I had found my life's calling.

The bottom line was that little Skylar Krum, who was probably as thin as my thigh, was a charming child. She did everything I told her to do, never questioning me or showing the least bit of reluctance. It was clear she really did want to learn the piano, which made my job a lot easier. But aside from that, she was a very disciplined and obedient five-year-old, which made me wonder if she ever had been cross in her short young life or given the Krums any problems at all. When she asked me if I would please give her homework, I wanted to lean down and give her a hug. Her innocence and eagerness to learn filled me with great hope and I could tell that she genuinely liked me as much as I liked her.

I remember not wanting to leave when our time was up. I couldn't believe how fast the hour had gone, and how much we had accomplished in our first lesson. Right at two o'clock, Jessica Krum opened the French doors and instructed her daughter to "thank Ms. Lauren because it is time for her to go." There was a small bit of whining, but I assured her I'd be back next week. And if she improved by the next lesson, I told her, I'd give her a bronze, silver or gold sticker, with the gold being the best.

"A gold sticker?" Skylar's eyes widened.

"Yes, sweetie. You could get a gold sticker. But you've got to practice for me, okay?"

Skylar nodded so hard her entire body shook. "Yes, ma'am. Can I practice today?"

"As long as your mom and dad say it's okay," I told her, not wanting to impose my authority where it wasn't welcome.

I made it a point to show Mrs. Krum the notebook we had started, which I explained would provide her and Mr. Krum, if he so desired, a weekly record of what we had worked on and instructions for Skylar's practicing. Jessica complimented me on this idea and told me it would be very helpful in keeping up with her progress. I didn't have a chance to explain to her that I was just following my mother's approach with her own students, because about that same time, Coach Krum came up behind us and asked how the lesson had gone.

"I think it went good," I said, turning to face him.

After a rather awkward pause during which our eyes met, he drew a folded envelope from his pocket. "Thank you again, Lauren," he said, holding it out to me. Seeing it there in his hand served as a blunt reminder that they were paying me for my services, and I suddenly felt embarrassed for taking money from them at all. I had had such a pleasant experience at their house that afternoon that I would have gone back for free. In fact, if Coach Krum had suggested so in the first place, I would have agreed to teach his daughter for absolutely no money at all.

Chapter 18

When I finally had a chance to talk to my mom about Skylar's lessons, she started digging through her box of sheet music, pulling out several selections that she told me would be perfect for Skylar.

"Here's 'London Bridge Is Falling Down.' You loved that one when you were little." A thin smile formed on my mother's face. "Oh, and here's another one—'Send in the Clowns.' You played it over and over and over."

She sat next to me on the carpet, her legs curled under her, thumbing through the same selections that she had used to teach me when I was a kid. Some were yellowed, but still in good shape. I moved closer to her and breathed in her light floral scent.

"You know, baby, you have a chance at this that I never had," she said, sounding frighteningly like my father. "I never had proper schooling in music, but you could. You could go all the way."

My mother had never gone to college, never had the opportunity; but her love for the piano had motivated her to make a career out of it anyway, even if it did only consist of teaching children in the neighborhood. I'm sure that at one time she'd had high hopes for herself, but my sister and I had sidelined her ambition, placing her securely in the heart of the home. It was by my father's pompous generosity that he allowed her to work at all. I wondered sometimes whether, if he had been a different breed of man, one who supported his wife's dreams as much as his own, doors might have opened up for my mother beyond the piano in our living room. But as I knelt over the box of sheet music with her, I realized that this would most likely never be possible now. She had no choice but to continue living a story that she otherwise wouldn't have written.

I wanted so badly to keep talking about the future and all its possibilities, but my father walked in and gave us a disapproving stare. At the sight of him, all energy drained from my mother's face. She scrambled to her feet and quickly made up a story about dropping the box and how I was helping her pick up its contents. But I guess he was onto us, because he repeated to her the warning he had given me: he would not tolerate my spending additional time on music outside my weekly lesson with the Krum child.

My mother found us a way around this rule, volunteering to drive me to and from Skylar's lessons as long as she didn't have any makeup lessons of her own that conflicted. We took advantage of every second in the car to discuss Skylar's progress and the things I could do as her teacher to keep her engaged. I don't know what I would have done without my mother's help, because after just three or four lessons, Skylar had already memorized most of the keys and was even playing a few simple combinations by memory. But even once I was sailing along nicely myself, I didn't want to give up my mother's attention. I'd come to crave that small gift of time on the way to the Krum's, when all we had to think about, to worry about, was eighty-eighty keys on an instrument that we both loved.

During Skylar's lessons I barely saw Coach Krum, except of course when it came time for him to pay me. He was clearly leaving the oversight of the lessons to his wife, though he would sometimes look in on Skylar and me during our time at the piano, careful not to alert his daughter to his presence. But I would know when he was there, and I would have to resist the urge to look back at him, even though I could feel his eyes burning through me from behind.

I also came to sense what I thought was Coach Krum's lingering focus on me during basketball practice. It seemed that whenever I'd steal a glance in his direction, he'd almost always be staring back at me with that signature boyish grin. Many nights I lay awake trying to convince myself that the glances were nothing more than a figment of my imagination. But when I found myself rummaging through my sister's makeup drawer, I realized that my feelings for him had shifted in a new direction. As I stood there looking ridiculous in my sister's purple eye shadow, I vowed to get off this path before I did something to embarrass myself, or worse, him.

I was completely resolved to this the afternoon my mom asked my sister to drive me to the Krums'. Carla threw an incredible fit about having to take me, complaining that it wasn't her problem that I didn't have a ride. It was nice to see my mom push back for once. She even raised her voice to Carla, telling her that she had no choice in the matter and that she'd also need to make herself available to pick me up at two.

When we got in the car, Carla flipped on the stereo so loud it nearly blasted me out of the vehicle. I could barely hear myself think, much less mentally prepare for Skylar's lesson. I couldn't speak with Carla either, which was fine by me. She seemed like a complete stranger next to me in the driver's seat, draped in black from head to toe right down to the polish on her fingernails. When she wasn't in her school uniform, she wore black, which was no doubt influenced by Shakey's dark and gloomy style.

I told her to drop me off a couple houses down from the Krums', not wanting them to hear her stereo at its ear-splitting volume or think that my sister was some fucked-up goth girl. Clearly it was mutual, as I had barely made it out of the car before she sped off—a cool reminder of her outright disgust for me. But I didn't let this bother me because I was off to a more cheerful place, even if it would be only for the next hour.

I rang the doorbell and waited. In the distance I could hear the buzzing of a lawnmower, but I couldn't tell from which yard it came. I didn't understand why it was taking so long for them to answer. The last couple of times, Skylar had answered the door, at first peering shyly behind it and then dashing toward me for a hug. Her mother had obviously given her permission to do this because she was always standing close by and observing her daughter's affection for me with what I took to be a look of indifference.

But that afternoon there was no Skylar to greet me at the door or Mrs. Krum to welcome me inside. I checked to see if my watch had stopped, but the second hand was still busily ticking away. Meanwhile the murmur of the lawnmower sounded like it was getting closer. I went down the steps and walked around to the side yard, and that's where I found Coach Krum pushing a mower.

Upon seeing me, he immediately switched off the motor and trotted over, shaking his head with a boyish grin on his face. "Oh Lauren, you're going to be very mad at me."

But I could never be mad at him for whatever it was, especially because of how attractive he looked laboring away in the yard. There was a ruggedness about him that didn't always come through at school, because there he was a teacher and a coach, and all that tended to be very intimidating. Seeing him in his gray sweatshirt and jeans made him seem more real to me and not so untouchable, almost like getting to know a celebrity outside his fame.

"I completely forget to tell you that Jessica took Skylar to see her grandparents this weekend."

Somewhere in the depths of me something lurched to life. I couldn't have been more pleased to hear him say this or more confused as to why it excited me so. "That's okay," I said, straining not to smile. "I can just wait on the porch for my sister."

"No, let me at least drive you home. I feel bad as it is."

I dug the toe of my sneakers into the grass. "Well, the thing is, I don't think she was going back home, so I wouldn't want her to make a trip back here for nothing."

He gave me a sideways glance and smiled. "Are ya hungry? 'Cause I just so happen to make the best bologna and cheese sandwich in these here parts."

I giggled at his exaggerated Texas twang. Out of the corner of my eye, I saw a grin flash across his face.

My body started trembling the moment I followed him inside. It had taken me a good week to recover from the last time I was alone with him in his house. The way he had tracked my every word, the way his eyes bored into mine, that had stayed with me for days. Now, just being alone with him again made my secret crush bubble up once more.

While he made the sandwiches, I sat nervously watching TV in the darkened living room. I left the television on the same station as I had found it—a college football game at low volume—and was careful not to open the blinds or mess up the loose papers strewn across the coffee table. The papers appeared to be diagrams of hand-drawn offensive plays, and just as I leaned in for a better look, Coach Krum emerged from the kitchen with a plate in either hand.

"I'm glad you're looking at those, because I might need your opinion."

I was relieved that he wasn't mad, since he had basically caught me snooping. "Um, sure."

Coach Krum plopped next to me on the couch. "I've been thinking that we need to work the baseline more." He fingered the pencil behind his ear. "We need to take advantage of your scrambling ability and Beth's quick dishes to the perimeter."

There was no doubt that Beth was brilliant at passing the ball at just the right moment, and he had a point about my speed. "Why not bring Emerson to the top of the perimeter and have either me or Beth fake a shot from the far sides?"

"That'll only work if we can bring Tracey up for the screen, and that would leave us thin under the basket for rebounds."

"So why not bring me or Beth, whoever's free, out for the screen. We could get there quicker and maybe cause a draw."

He sat there pondering my suggestion as he rubbed his hand over his cheeks and mouth. We were sitting so near to each other that I could hear his palm move over the bristles of his unshaven skin. I could smell the outdoors on him; grass clippings, dust and a bag of freshly raked leaves.

As we continued to discuss the diagrams, he stood up, removed his sweatshirt and sat down next to me again, this time so close that our thighs actually touched. He still had his undershirt on, but it fit him so snugly that I couldn't help noticing the outline of his chest muscles and the hair peeking out from under his shirt. As my breath quickened, I felt myself looking over the edge and wanting to know more than ever what it'd be like to free-fall.

And fall I did. The next few moments shot past me in a blur. We moved the coffee table out of the way and started walking through the different plays we'd discussed only minutes before. Then things got playful. Whether I initiated it or he did, I can't really say. All I know is that suddenly we were having a full-out basketball game, trying to maneuver past each other to dunk wadded pieces of paper in a nearby clothes basket. There was a lot of pushing and grabbing going on, and before I knew it, we were wrestling on the couch with him on top of me.

This next part is difficult for me to talk about because it marks the point at which our relationship as coach and player, teacher and student, crossed the line. I could lie and tell you that I didn't expect it, but deep down I knew it was coming, and I knew I wouldn't say no. At fifteen, I didn't know the meaning of the word no. It wasn't in my range of competency, or at least I didn't feel like I deserved it to be. I was comfortable with being directed, being controlled, being told what to do. So as Coach Krum pinned my arms on either side of me . . . as his lips pressed against mine . . . and as his tongue found its way into my mouth, I traded any choice I had, for his.

Yet even so, something in my gut told me that what we were doing on his couch, the very couch where his wife and little girl probably sat, was terribly, terribly wrong. But I didn't try to stop him, even when the voice inside my head was screaming for me to do so. Instead I froze and lay there, probably more from fear than anything else, I now realize, while he moved his hands over my body. And slowly the screaming inside me subsided as I felt myself sink into a dimension I hadn't known existed. If it hadn't been for my sister's honking of the horn to interrupt us, who knows how far things might have gone, because in his arms that day I was utterly defenseless, shackled and bound by the way he touched me and imprisoned by the very sound of his voice.

Some people told me later that what happened that day was abuse, though never once did I see it that way. But what did I know of abuse? Didn't every kid have to hide in closets when her parents fought? Didn't other dads hit their wives? Did it not say in the Bible for a wife to love and obey her husband? At least what happened on the couch that day didn't involve any yelling or hitting.

       After that first encounter with Daniel, I spent a considerable amount of time in front of the bathroom mirror, straining to see if I looked any different or more grown-up. With the exception of the beard burn around my lips where he had kissed me so hard, I looked exactly the same—same thin face, same pale skin and same mousy brown hair. Underneath it all, though, I had changed. Kissing Daniel Krum had plucked me out of my small, insignificant world and placed me in an entirely different one. The thought of it made me cower with embarrassment, tremble with fear, and squeal with giddiness all at once.

Chapter 19

He told me it was the dress, the red dress I wore to the homecoming dance that had made him unable to resist me. He disclosed this to me later over the phone that same day we kissed, calling me on my line well past midnight.

When the phone rang I was still awake, not wanting or even able to fall asleep. My encounter with Coach Krum earlier that day had left me as numb and spaced-out as if I had done drugs for the first time. And really, I had in a way; I had snorted him like cocaine, up my nose and through my body, and then up, up I had ridden to the sky, where I floated above the earth, only to free-fall into his arms. And now . . . now there were no arms to break my fall . . . falling down now . . . down, down, spiraling down, tumbling down, back to ground zero.

But free falling into love was the least of my worries. I had real problems, like people finding out that I kissed my coach and losing my spot on the team.

As I lay there slowly being crushed under my own shame, my sister barged into my room. Even though it was close to one o'clock in the morning, she was still dressed as if she was going out, which tipped me off that she'd later be making a trip out her bedroom window. "There's a guy on the phone for you," she said blankly. I told her to tell Fisher I didn't feel like talking, but she informed me that it wasn't Fisher, and if I didn't hurry to the phone she would hang up on the guy and I would never know which dork was calling me now.

My hands were shaking so violently that I could hardly hold the phone cord in place on the receiver. I waited until my sister hung up before I said hello, pleading with God that no one was calling to inform me I was being expelled.

"Lauren, this is Daniel."

I remember being so caught off guard when he identified himself by his first name that I let too much time lapse. He must have thought I'd hung up.

"Are you still there?"

I bit down hard on my finger. "Yes, yes, I'm sorry."

"Well, I don't blame you if you don't want to talk to me."

I was struck by this, almost convinced that I had heard him incorrectly. But at the same time, I was incredibly relieved. I felt as if he had just told me I'd been cured of a fatal disease.

"No, Coach, I do want to talk to you."

There was an awkward pause, and for a moment I thought I had lost him. "Coach Krum?"

"Lauren, please don't call me that." His voice trailed off. "It's Daniel. It's just Daniel from now on."

And so from that point forward, he was just Daniel to me, at least when we were alone. That night he told me he mainly called to make sure I was all right. We never discussed the consequences of what had happened, but we didn't say it wouldn't ever happen again, either. He explained to me that two people are sometimes brought together by a force greater than themselves. He made it all sound very romantic, and by the time we'd been on the phone for nearly two hours, I was lapping up every word he spoke, like a person dying of thirst.

And I was dying of thirst. I had been for a long time. As the hours ticked by that night and I heard my sister leave and then return again through her window, I felt a sense of healing come over me just from listening to the sound of his voice. He was so easy to talk to that as fatigue set in for both of us, the silent gaps in our conversation didn't bother me or compel me to find another topic to discuss just for the sake of talking. I got the feeling he found it easy being on the phone with me too, because he told me everything about himself: everything from growing up in a military family to spending his high school years in the harsh winters of Wisconsin. I also found out, over the course of our conversation, that he had played basketball for a small college in Minnesota, but hadn't been good enough to make it to the pros.

"That's all I dreamed of for years," he told me, an echo of regret in his voice. "But when it didn't happen for me, I didn't have anything else lined up . . . and, well, Jessica wanted to get married, so I decided to go into coaching."

Hearing him speak her name made my stomach flip, but I didn't want him to know how much it bothered me. I quickly changed the subject.

"Are you happy with your choice?"

"To marry Jessica?"

My breath hitched. "No, no, with coaching."

"Oh, sure. It kept me in the game. And it's a good living, if you want to look at it that way. But ..."

"It's still not the same as playing?"

"No, it's not the same as playing. I mean, watching you girls juke and score, there's nothing like it, you know, to be able to do that yourself. But there's always that one player who's so good and easy to coach that you feel you're playing through her. I think you know who I'm talking about."

I did know, but I was too paralyzed by his words to respond.

"There's just something different about you, Lauren. I feel like I can tell you anything. You are a very special young woman and I won't let you get hurt."

And I believed him. I believed that he thought I was special and that he wouldn't let anything happen to me. For the first time in my life, I wanted to set aside all my worries and let someone else take them. On that night and on many more nights, he was that person—the person I wanted to rescue me.

As dawn broke through the curtains in my room, we agreed that perhaps it was time to get some sleep. He mentioned that "they" (meaning his wife and daughter) would be home from their trip in the afternoon, and that he had plenty of chores to get done before then. But when we hung up shortly afterward, there was an understanding that this wasn't the end, but rather the beginning—words that still ring fresh in my mind.

"Lauren, I don't want to hang up."

"I don't, either."

"I want so badly to kiss you again," he said.

"You do?"

"Yes, I do very much. Is that okay?"

I realized my hands were shaking. "Yes, it's okay, but what if someone finds out?"

"No one will find out, because I won't let that happen. This is our special secret. Don't you trust me?"

"Of course I do."

"Are you sure you're going to be okay, then?"

"Yes, I'm sure."

"Lauren?"

"Yes?"

"I want you to know that you are very special to me."

Chapter 20

Not for a minute did I consider telling anyone about what had happened between me and Daniel Krum. I had no knowledge about indecency with a child laws or any other statute protecting minors from sexual predators. But even if I had, I probably wouldn't have seen any correlation whatsoever, despite the fact that he was thirty-five and I was fifteen.

I had kissed him back. I'd not stopped his hand when he moved it over me. I wanted him just as badly as he wanted me. And honestly, I didn't want the feeling of exhilaration to end, either. I knew that if I told anyone, even June, the bubble that held my make-believe romance would burst, and I'd lose it forever. I was desperate to protect it, this secret love of mine. That's how real it was to me. I couldn't eat, I couldn't sleep and by no means could I concentrate. All I could think about was him and the next time we could be alone. I planned, I conspired, I thought of every way possible we could make this work, and not once did I assume that he wasn't thinking the same.

At school, almost as if by unspoken conspiracy, we were careful to carry on as we usually did as coach and player, though not without giving each other an occasional glance of interest. During practice, he'd make a point of standing nearer to me or finding reasons to touch me in some way, taking me by the hips and moving me to the appropriate position during a walk-through of a play or squeezing my shoulder for a job well done.

He did this all very subtly, careful not to tip off the other players as to what was going on. I did my best to remain neutral around him too, but it got harder as the days wore on and the tension between us built. My yearning for him was breaking me down, and at times it became so profound that if he even grazed my skin, what felt like shock waves would travel through my body.

Seeing Daniel on a daily basis gave me a renewed interested in my appearance. I no longer wanted to arrive at school without makeup, which I'm sure most of my fellow classmates would have considered odd given that Saint Agnes was an all-girls institution. I also started wearing my hair down and smoothed at my shoulders more often, taking more time in the morning than usual to blow it dry and pulling it up in a ponytail only when it was necessary for practice. I didn't have any makeup of my own, so I took to swiping items from Carla's drawer, telling myself that she had more than enough and most likely wouldn't miss the few bits and pieces I borrowed.

Unfortunately, my new polished look caught the attention not only of Daniel but also of Carla, June and a few of the girls on the team. The latter just ribbed me about it, nicknaming me "beauty queen" and joking that if I got too sweaty, I might melt. I could handle their teasing, but I couldn't handle the way Carla called me out at breakfast on a morning when my dad was already about to blow.

It all started with the eggs. My dad claimed that he asked for "fried," but my mom had heard something else. Despite her apology, he snatched the plate out of her hands. "Never mind. I don't have time to wait for you to get my breakfast right."

My mom turned slowly and went back to sink. She started scrubbing the dishes, but then her shoulders slumped and her head bent lower, and she placed a hand on the counter. That's when Carla waltzed in, poured some cereal and milk in a bowl and plopped down at the table.

"So Güera, what made you decide to start wearing makeup?"

My father cleared his throat and glared at us over his reading glasses.

"I'm not wearing makeup."

"Oh okay, so what's that on your eyes?"

I gritted my teeth. "I said I'm *not* wearing any."

"Liar."

My father slammed his fork on his plate. I froze. "Carla, leave your sister alone!" There was a vicious edge to his voice.

Carla rolled her eyes. "You always take her side!"

My father shot up from his chair and glared at my sister from across the table. "You better watch your tone with me!" By this point, my mother was tugging on his arm.

Carla shoved her chair back from the table. "Did you even know that she has a *boyfriend?*"

All color drained from my father's face. His eyes shifted from Carla to me.

"That's right," Carla said. "Lauren has a boyfriend. In fact, he called for her last night. Sam, is it?"

"I don't know a Sam." Through pursed lips I mouthed, "Stop." I felt my father's missile lock on me.

"Is there a boy calling you, Lauren?" My eyes jumped back to him. "I've told you before that you're too young to be dating."

"No boy is calling me, Dad."

"Oh my God, are you kidding me?" Carla said. "A guy called for you last night. You even came in my room demanding what time he had called."

"Is this true, Lauren?" my dad said.

"No."

He glared Carla. "Is this one of your tricks?"

"For crying out loud, Carl," my sister snarled. "Why would I even waste my time?"

"Don't you call me Carl! I'm your father!"

"Okay, *Dad*. Whatever you say, *Dad*."

"Watch your tone with me, young lady!"

"Or what? You'll hit me like you do mom?"

Five . . . four . . . three . . . two . . . one.

The bomb split apart; shrapnel flew everywhere, and when the dust settled, my father's hands were around my sister's throat.

"That's enough! You don't speak to me that way, you hear me?"

I saw the whites of my dad's eyes. A searing white. The hottest part of the flame.

That's when she sprung on his back, my mother, like a feral cat. She dug her nails into his face and opened his eyelid. The blood flowed. He cried out, let go of Carla and threw my mom off of his back and onto the floor. Then after finding his balance, he leaned over her and backhanded her across the face.

"I fucking hate you!"

My father swung around ready to spring, ready to fight at my sister's words. I hooked my arms around Carla's and held them behind her back. She fought me to get at him. She kept saying over and over that she hoped he'd die. So I held her tighter, because I wanted her to live.

"You're just like your mother . . . good for nothing." My father wiped the blood from his eyelid and left the room.

My mother lay curled on the floor. Her hands covered her face, and she looked as if she was laughing. But she wasn't laughing, she was crying.

Chapter 21

Later that morning as I sat in Sister Judith Ann's geometry class, all I could think about was how the bits of scrambled eggs had scattered over the kitchen floor. The real fucked-up thing about having a father like mine was that the minute the ground stopped moving and the shards of glass were swept up, everything would go back to the way it had been before. My dad would go to work, my sister and I to school and my mother would go to her bedroom and redo her makeup. It was a scary normal, an unnatural one in which nobody dared mention the screaming and backhanding, the blood and the eggs mixed up together on the linoleum floor.

That evening my father came into my room, wearing a butterfly bandage across his eyelid. It still was crusted over with blood, though I didn't ask him about it. In fact I said nothing to him until he cleared his throat and spoke first.

"You got a home game this week?"

"Uh, yeah. I think."

"Thursday?"

"Yeah."

"Okay, I'll be there."

On the day of the game, I took my time walking to and from class, lingering in the halls more than usual. I just didn't want the school day to end; I was dreading having to suit up for the game and deal with my father carrying on like a maniac from the bleachers. He'd long taken the fun out of basketball for me. The moment he'd start his heckling, I'd be back on that driveway again, throwing up bricks and air balls in time with his excessive verbal beat downs.

And sure enough, barely a minute had come off the clock that night when my dad started hollering at me to pass the ball quicker, hustle more and get my head in the game.

"Dude, does your dad ever shut up?" Beth passed the ball in to me and we started down the court.

She had no idea. "No," I said, rolling my eyes. "He's always like this."

As I brought the ball to the half-court line, I saw the other players turn and look in his direction. I could tell by their expressions that they were less than pleased. And then out of nowhere, I heard Beth holler, "Wolf!" and by the time I registered what she meant, one of the players from the other team had snatched the ball out of my hands and driven it down the other way for an easy basket.

Damn it to hell. Now we were down by ten, and my father was exploding at me from the stands.

Daniel, or Coach Krum, rather, called a time-out, took me aside and looked me in the eye. "Let's take a deep breath for a second. I know he's driving you crazy."

"I can't do this with him here!" The pressure built behind my eyes and they began welling with tears. I rubbed at them and hoped he didn't think I was being too childish.

Instead, he moved his face closer to mine and I felt his sweaty palm touch my cheek. "Yes you can, because I'm going to take care of it at halftime." His voice was steady and firm. "Just let it go and leave it to me. If he starts to get to you, just look over at me and I'll be out there with you."   There were several times during the remainder of the quarter where I did look over in Daniel's direction. And just like he said, his eyes were there to welcome me and remind me that I was no longer fighting this alone. For the first time, I felt protected. I actually felt safe.

Coach Krum was gone for most of halftime, leaving the team idle in the locker room. No one talked to me, not even Beth. I think they were all too astounded—and too annoyed—to know what to say. We were losing because of my father, which made me an easy target for their frustration. I was relieved when Daniel finally joined us in the locker room.

"Why does everyone look so glum?" he asked, glancing around at all of us slumped on the benches. "The problem's been taken care of, and we've got a game to win. Now get your butts back on the court!"

I never got a chance to ask him what he said to my father that day. Whatever it was worked, because my dad was nowhere to be found by the start of the second half. And from the reassuring glance Daniel gave me as we trotted onto the court, I knew my father wouldn't ever be a problem at my games again.

We ended up coming from behind for the win, with me dishing out a career-high twenty-six points. This of course made me the hero of the game, earning me plenty of praise from my teammates, including even Emerson and Beth. The person I really wanted praise from was Daniel, but he kept his distance and let the girls fuss over me. Finally I realized that I wasn't going to get any alone time with him. I needed to figure out a way home anyway, so reluctantly I decided to look for my father. I hadn't seen him since the start of halftime.

Through the veil of fog blanketing the parking lot, I spotted my father's blue Skylark sitting under the lamp. It took everything in me not to run as I approached the car. What was he going to do to me once I got in and closed the door? I had seen what he was capable of with my mother, and now that I was getting older, I sometimes worried, especially on days when he seemed more on edge than usual, that it was only a matter of time before he'd raise a hand to me. He certainly hadn't hesitated when Carla and I were little. And he definitely didn't hesitate when he wrapped his hands around Carla's throat.

Just as I was about to open the car door, I heard Daniel call my name. I turned and saw him jogging toward me, and as he got closer, I was comforted by his warm smile.

"Just wanted to make sure everything was okay," he said cheerfully, opening the door for me and leaning over to address my father. "Carl, how are we doing?"

"Fine, Coach, just fine." My father gave him several exaggerated nods.

"She played a hell of a game tonight. You should be very proud of her."

"Yes, I'm proud . . . you can be sure of that."

"Well, good. I'm glad to hear we're on the same page, because I'd be very disappointed if I heard different."

"No, Coach, you won't hear anything different."

"Okay then," he said, straightening up beside me and placing his hand on the small of my back. "Lauren, again—nice job. I'll see you at practice tomorrow."

Chapter 22

Thanks to whatever it was Daniel told my father, he didn't speak a cross word to me that night on the way home or for several nights after that. I felt like I had just been awarded a bodyguard, someone to shield me from the storm that was my father.

Even if my father had shouted at me all the way home, it wouldn't have mattered. I was too swept away by my feelings for Daniel—and from the high of winning the game. But when I didn't get a call from Daniel that night, my excitement quickly fizzled. And then a week went by and I still hadn't heard from him, and I started to think that he'd changed his mind. Perhaps a night alone with his wife in their bed had convinced him otherwise—convinced him that someone like me just wasn't worth it, and why in God's name was he putting everything at risk?

Daniel wasn't around for Skylar's lesson that week or the one after that. I had thought about canceling the lessons altogether, but that would have made it obvious that I was taking what had happened between Daniel and me way too hard. So as usual, I swallowed my pride and my dignity when Jessica Krum invited me inside on that following Saturday. I was careful to keep my distance and act casual, hoping that she wouldn't pick up on the crush I had on her husband. She looked flawless in her shoulder pads and pleated slacks, gliding across the room on dainty feet. I felt like a clumsy giraffe loping along behind her.

To make things worse, she seemed overly eager to connect with me that day. It was almost to the point of being fake, the way she asked me how the season was going, and what it was like to be at a new school. Her sudden interest in me made me extremely anxious, especially when she paused momentarily in front of the very couch where Daniel and I had kissed. It wasn't until Skylar and I were safely behind closed doors and free to start our lesson that I stopped trembling.

As Skylar started to play, the muscles in my neck and shoulders slowly relaxed. I was finally in my element, in a place where no one could touch me—at least for the moment. I soon got swept up in Skylar's little world, all giggles and smiles as she pounded out the "Itsy Bitsy Spider." Her fingering was wrong and she looked like she was typing, but I didn't dare correct her. Not when she was having so much fun. She was a kitten playing with a ball of yarn, a bird on a wing learning to fly. I almost felt guilty when I switched her over to a site-reading exercise. She looked up at me and whined, and how could I blame her? I hated sight reading, too.

"Hey girlie, do you wanna take a break?"

She nodded so hard she nearly fell off the bench.

"Do you want me to play something for you?"

This time Skylar shook her head, got up and walked to the oversize chair near the window. Then she knelt on the floor and pulled out a pair of Raggedy Ann and Andy dolls from behind the chair.

"My daddy got these for me," she said, holding them out and then pulling them into her body in a tight hug. "He plays them with me."

I smiled at this, but then realized that at Skylar's age, I couldn't have said the same. My dad had never played with me.

"What do you play?"

"We play wedding." She held the dolls in front of her and made them walk down an imaginary aisle.

"What their names?"

"Daddy and Lauren."

That's when little Skylar made the two dolls kiss, smashing their faces together. I sat there in horror as she continued to make them kiss over and over and over again.

"No, no, that can't be Lauren," I said, pointing to the Raggedy Ann doll. "That's your mommy."

"No, it's you!" she said, giggling. "Mommy's mad at Daddy."

Why was Skylar doing this? Did she know?

After that, I thought I was going to throw up. I quickly excused myself and went into the guest bathroom. I splashed water on my face and willed myself to keep it together. When I came out a few minutes later, I found the entire Krum family sitting in the living room. Jessica jumped up when she saw me.

"Lauren, are you feeling okay? You don't look so good?"

"I'm fine, thanks," I said. My voice cracked and I pretended to cough.

"Do you want me to get you a glass of water or something?"

I looked at the floor and shook my head. I knew if our eyes met, I wouldn't be able to hold back a sob. I just wanted to get out of there.

I was relieved when Daniel handed me an envelope. I took it without looking at him, even though I could sense that he was fishing for my eyes. I'm not sure if I even said goodbye as I slipped out the front door and bounded down the steps to my mother's waiting car.

I didn't open the envelope until later that afternoon, right before Fisher was scheduled to arrive. Yes, that's right; I ended up inviting Fisher over to meet my parents. It was the only way I knew to distract them from what was really going on, a cover-up of sorts to keep the appearance of honesty in at least one area of my life. But I was dreading every minute of it, even though I had made it very clear to Fisher that his visit meant nothing and that the only reason I was even allowing him to come over was that my sister had run her mouth to my dad about a boy calling me. Fisher didn't seem to have a problem with that; he'd even asked if Carla was going to be home, too. I'd told him I wasn't sure, but to be my guest to pester her all he wanted.

A few minutes before he came over, I hurriedly opened the envelope from Daniel Krum. When I pulled out the ten-dollar bill, though, a note fell out on the floor. I could barely read it because I was shaking so hard.

Lauren,

I can't get you out of my head. I'll figure out a
way to call you tonight.

Daniel

It was a short note, but one that gave me great hope that
his feelings for me hadn't changed. I read it over as many times as
I could, dissecting it down to individual words, searching for an
underlying meaning that could tell me more. When the doorbell
rang, I thought of every reason not to answer it, but when it rang
a second time, my mother called to me from the kitchen to let the
boy in.

Surprisingly, Fisher was on his best behavior, although he
scarfed down the pizza as if he hadn't eaten in days. His lack of
table manners didn't seem to bother my dad, though. He
appeared more interested in listening to Fisher talk about the
Latin classes that the boys from Memorial were required to take.
I guess my lecturing Fisher on topics that were acceptable to
bring up to my father paid off, because by the end of dinner, he
had managed to win my dad's interest in the Memorial Honor
Code, which, according to Fisher, all students—including
himself—took very seriously.

"More schools should have honor codes like that," my
father said.

"Dad," I said, trying to get a word in. "Saint Agnes has an
honor code, too . . . not just Memorial."

"You know, Lauren, I'm kinda glad you met this here
Fisher." He put his arm around Fisher as if he were his son.
"Seems like he's the kind of Christian boy I'd want you to be
around."

I wanted to slit my wrists rather than agree with him, but
I knew I'd better just nod and be done with it so Fisher's visit
could end as soon as possible. As for Fisher, when he heard my
father's comment, he gave me a most sickening look that told me
there wasn't a Christian bone in him. But he had proved to be a
good actor and was playing my father brilliantly, and for that I
was grateful. Still, it didn't make it any easier for me to stomach

him looking me up and down. There was only one person I welcomed doing that, and I'd be expecting his call later that evening.

I got a brief reprieve from Fisher's nonsense when Carla emerged from her room. She was obviously going out, given the way she was dressed in black, with her long, dark hair teased high at the bangs and her blood-red lipstick that made her look like a vampire. And just like that, I was invisible, which suited me fine. Fisher practically stumbled over himself getting up to shake her hand, which she didn't give to him until my father barked at her to stop being so rude. Fisher was absolutely dumbstruck by her, which most guys were, and for a moment I wondered if I had the same effect on Daniel.

But certainly not, I thought to myself as Fisher panted away at my sister. I wasn't pretty enough to cast a spell over someone like she could. And as I made a mental note to never let my sister meet Daniel, she turned to me and said she had left a phone message on my bed.

Fuck. I really needed to get Fisher out of my house.

"Man, that practice this morning is hitting me," I said, accompanying my words with an extra-big yawn. "I think I'm gonna turn in."

When I walked Fisher to the door out of earshot of my parents, he stood there in the foyer as if expecting something. "Well?" he said, folding his arms.

"I told you that this doesn't mean a thing!" I hissed.

"Don't worry, I remember what you said . . . but we had a deal, sweetie, so pay up."

I had been so caught up in not wanting to miss Daniel's call that I had completely forgotten about my agreement with Fisher. "Fine. Stay here."

I came back from my room carrying a brown paper sack that was folded and stapled at the opening. "Here," I said, shoving it in his coat. "Just like you asked."

"Unwashed?"

"Yes, unwashed."

God, what a pervert. You would think I'd have been horrified at the thought of giving a pair of dirty underwear to Fisher, but I really could not have cared less. I was already

distracted enough by the prospect of Daniel calling; and given the
fact that the pair of red satin panties I was sending home with
Fisher belonged to my sister (which I made clear to him), I wasn't
at all compelled to worry myself about it. He got what he wanted
and so did I.

  The thing that was bothering me, though, was trying to
figure out when the hell Daniel would call. With my sister gone
for the evening, it would be easy for me to talk on the phone, but
once she returned at curfew, my phone time would be limited. I
also couldn't figure out who had called for me earlier. The note
Carla had left me simply read "Sam called. Will call back." I was
relieved to know that it hadn't been Daniel—that I hadn't really
missed his call. Plus it unnerved me a bit to think of him talking
to my sister and leaving his name. Not that she knew a thing
about my coach, but she could easily have let his name slip at the
dinner table and complicate things even more.

Chapter 23

When I finally got a call from Daniel that night, he told me that he had in fact phoned earlier in the evening, using "Sam" as his code name.

"I can tell that you and your sister are nothing alike," he said. He was calling me from the phone in his work shed, located several yards from the house in the back corner of the yard, but he still spoke in a quiet tone. He told me he often went out there when he wanted to watch films or work on plays, or when he just couldn't sleep.

"How's that?" I asked, nervous at the mention of my sister.

"She doesn't give off the warmth that you do. But then again, I don't know many people who can."

And I believed him. Never before had I felt so special, so *loveable* to another person. There were several times during our conversation when he told me similar things, each time making it easier for me to fall for him. He was so much more eloquent in this way than me, and when he admitted that he could be overly emotional and hoped that side of him wouldn't scare me off, I wanted to reach for him through the phone and never let go.

In fact, I was crushing so hard that if he had asked me to run away with him, I would have packed my bags and followed him to the other side of the world.

And it seemed like I wasn't the only one who thought so. "You didn't seem yourself this afternoon, Lauren. I was afraid that maybe your feelings had changed."

I hadn't expected him to ask me this. I didn't know he'd been watching me so closely. "I thought *your* feelings had changed," I said. "When I didn't hear from you all week, I thought the worst."

"Lauren, I just don't go around doing this all the time. In fact, I've never done this, and that's why it's scaring me so much."

Because he had been so open with me, I felt comfortable telling him that I was scared, too. I told him the whole thing about Skylar and her dolls, and why it had made me so jumpy. I was careful not to place any blame on the child, though, knowing how much his daughter meant to him.

"That's no reason to get nervous," he said, assuring me there was no way Skylar could have found out, much less pieced it together. "We have nothing to worry about . . . kids will be kids, Lauren. I guess I probably talk about you a little too much, and her young imagination ran from there. And she likes you just so dang much. She told me she wants to be like 'Miss Lauren' when she grows up."

She wants to be like Miss Lauren when she grows up.

I'll admit this gave me pause, but it would be weeks before I'd fully realize the deeper meaning of his statement. At the time I was too lost in my obsession for him to see anything past our make-believe courtship; too mesmerized to recognize the lives we would affect; and too naïve to believe that the idea of him and me—together—could possible work out to a happily ever after.

•••

Over the next couple of weeks, we kept the charade going as best we could, being ever so careful not to get caught. He'd call me on random nights when his wife fell asleep before he did, and he kept passing me notes some Saturdays. It became more difficult to hide our feelings during basketball practice, and on one or two occasions I could have sworn that Emerson saw us exchange smiles.

She seemed to always be watching me now with that condescending smirk of hers, or at least that's what I assumed. Daniel assured me I was just being paranoid, but I couldn't get the idea out of my head that maybe she was onto us, that maybe she saw something that we were completely blind to. But in the end he convinced me to stop worrying about things that probably would never come to pass. And with my eyes squeezed shut, I agreed to trust him.

He called me that night. "I need to see you again," he said.

I pictured him leaning in close to me.

"Real soon," he added.

I bit down on my knuckle and drew blood.

"My office. In the weight room. When's your free period?"

The plan was to meet at ten o'clock Wednesday between my geometry and European history classes. We'd have the weight room and the gym all to ourselves, but I'd have to wait four days—four whole days until I could feel his arms around me and taste his lips on mine. I had taken that first hit, and now I wanted more.

When the sun streamed into my room that Wednesday morning, I'd already been up for hours. I was working on my breathing . . . inhale, one, two, three, exhale, one, two, three. But even all that practice didn't do me any good. By the time geometry rolled around, I was shaking so hard that the shape on my paper looked like the Mixmaster on the LBJ Freeway and Highway 75 rather than an isosceles trapezoid.

The bell rang and I shot out of my chair like a horse out of the starting gate. I made a pit stop in the bathroom, where I hid behind a stall and awkwardly applied some blush and lip gloss. Would he like the taste of the lip gloss? I wondered. Bubble gum cherry? Did his wife wear lip gloss? Had I lost my mind?

By the time I reached the gym, I had bigger issues on my mind than the flavor of my lip gloss. Thoughts were flooding my head: *Why is my blouse so wet under my armpits and what if someone sees us and oh my God, what the hell am I going to do once I get inside his office?*

When I saw the light spilling out of his office door, I nearly turned and ran. Then I heard someone behind me. "I thought maybe you'd changed your mind."

There was Daniel in a sport coat, khakis and a tie, holding a cup of coffee and wearing a boyish grin. I pawed the floor with my shoe and shook my head. I couldn't keep the side of my mouth from drawing up to my eyes. He brushed past me into his office, grazing my arm. An aromatic mix of coffee grounds and pine trees lingered in the air. I followed.

His grin got bigger as he slowly and very methodically closed the door behind me. The snap of the steel latch made me jump. He moved closer and took my hand. My chest rose and fell sharply. I didn't want what I wanted; I wanted what I shouldn't want. I gulped down a deep breath.

"Are you okay?" He took my face into his hands and gently placed his mouth over mine.

Bombs went off, but not the kind that sent me running for cover in my closet. No, this one was different. It wasn't about fight, it wasn't about flight; it was about getting more of him, all of him. Already his lips were on mine, and still it seemed like it would never be enough.

His hands broke away from my cheeks and moved downward now, spilling down my chest, down still further, resting for a moment on my hip. I was surprised he didn't spend more time on my breasts, but then again, he had already felt them one time before, and he was no teenage boy.

His next move would certainly prove that.

Being touched for the first time was a mind-blowing experience. I wondered for some time whether if that first touch had come from someone like Fisher, it would have had the same effect on me. But I think not. No boy can mimic the sexual prowess of a man, and I think it's fair to say that Daniel Krum probably had had numerous sexual escapades in his lifetime, because he knew exactly where and how to touch me to drive me crazy.

Don't think for a second, though that I tore off my clothes and rode him like a whore. The scene in his office that day would have seemed very tame to someone of experience. But to a fifteen-year-old girl, it might as well have been hardcore porn. He lifted my skirt and slid his hand along the outside of my thigh. Then he found his way under my panties and stroked me gently. I closed my eyes, but in the instant that the urge came over me to move with his fingers, his office phone rang and hurtled us back to the here and now—back to Lauren the student and Daniel the teacher. I pulled away from him and started straightening my school uniform as he leaned over the desk to answer the phone.

And that was it. I could tell by the formal tone of his voice that the person on the other line was someone of importance, so I decided it was best to leave at once. But for at least an hour after our time together in his office, I felt as if I had come down with a fever, because I couldn't stop perspiring. It was only after I walked outside without my coat that I finally could feel myself cool down in the frigid temperature of the afternoon.

That night over the phone, Daniel told me that he was afraid his actions had upset me—that his aggressive moves had scared me off. I assured him that this couldn't be further from the truth; in fact, I was sorry that our time together had run out so soon.

But did I really understand the true meaning of what I was saying to him? Did I understand that to a man this statement could mean it was okay for him to do more? Perhaps I did want more, but at no point did I ever consciously think about how far the physical part of our relationship might go. I honestly thought, and please believe me when I say this, that it would be nothing more than the heavy petting and kissing that had gone on in his office when the shades were drawn and the door was closed.

If only I hadn't been so blind.

Chapter 24

After the encounter in his office, things between Daniel and me heated up. He somehow managed to sneak away from his wife to call me three nights in a row, including the night of the away game that didn't put us back on campus until well after ten o'clock. We had a team van that he always drove to and from the games, and lately I had made it a point to find a seat in the very back to make sure I was giving none of my teammates a reason to get suspicious. In fact, I stayed as far away from him as I could, outside of what was considered normal interaction, because I was so paranoid of someone discovering the truth. But when we'd arrive back at school and all the girls would file out of the van, I'd stall and act like I was looking for something in my bag, just so I could linger a little while longer in his presence.

Maybe no one noticed, but Daniel did. He would tell me that he liked it when I did this, saying that it reassured him that I loved being with him just as much as he loved being with me. Although I didn't realize it at the time, I spent a considerable amount of effort convincing him that my feelings had not changed and never would. His insecurity was flattering to me then, but now I wonder if he was in fact testing my loyalty— testing to see if I'd blow the whistle on him. But back then that thought never crossed my mind.

My fire for him was consuming me and burning out my capacity for anything else. My grades started suffering, mostly because I was so exhausted all the time. Spending my nights talking to Daniel on the phone was keeping me up late, and when I wasn't talking to him, I was thinking about him. Even basketball began to slip; I no longer cared about beating everyone to the line in suicides, and Daniel started using Beth in more plays at point guard because of my clumsy mistakes. My head just wasn't in the game. It wasn't anywhere, except with Daniel Krum.

My head was so full of him, I didn't have even the capacity to keep up my friendship with June. I couldn't remember the last time we had talked on the phone for more than ten minutes. She had grown distant, not really saying much to me in the mornings when she'd pick me up for school. I asked her lots of questions about Jeremy, her parents or her brother, just so I could steer the focus away from me. She seemed to be doing fine without me at Pope Pius, anyway, taking more advanced placement classes than ever and making a new circle of friends. This might have bothered me if I hadn't been so preoccupied, but at that point I had more than enough drama in my life. I didn't have time to worry about my best friend moving on without me.

Truth be told, my involvement with Daniel Krum made me forget about a lot of things in my life, including the cold and stale environment in which I lived. Having him to focus on eased some of the grief I carried for my parents and the tumultuous relationships that had slowly chipped away at me through the years. I still got nervous around my family, but all that was getting easier. My world had shifted, opening my eyes to a more peaceful existence—one free of anger and strife, pain and resentment.

And so it was that my affair with Daniel Krum became my drug. I call it an affair, because at the time that's what I thought it was: forbidden love, like Romeo and Juliet. Like Hester Prynne and Reverend Dimmesdale. I was tangled up in the romance of it all, the late night calls, the stolen kisses, the touching, the breathing, the rapid-fire beating of my heart. I didn't care how I got it, I just wanted more; and never once did I consider the possibility of one day having to give it up. But then again, there were a lot of possibilities I didn't examine closely during that time of my life, many of which had consequences that a teenager could only dare to imagine.

I think about consequences a lot these days and wonder whether if I had had the luxury of hindsight, I would have ended up making my choices more carefully. There's really no way to answer this. At one point I think the idea of being with Daniel possessed me entirely; hell, sometimes it still does. Back then, I was such easy prey, such a brittle young soul, with a heart loosely held together with bits of Scotch tape and glue.

So even with the gift of retrospection, I probably would still have agreed to arrive at his house at one o'clock that following Saturday, though Jessica had pushed back Skylar's weekly lesson to two. They had a birthday party to attend, Daniel had told me, which meant we would have a rare opportunity to be completely *alone*. I remember the way he emphasized the words and how I lost my breath and how I just wanted one more, two more . . . *sigh* . . . many more minutes with him.

I showered quickly after practice on Saturday morning and hurriedly applied some of my sister's makeup and perfume. I had arranged for my father to drop me off and my mother to pick me up, hoping that no one would figure out that my time at the Krum house would span two hours instead of just one. It was easy to tell my dad one thing (the Krums needed to move Skylar's lesson up an hour) and my mom another (Skylar's lesson was moved back an hour). It was highly unlikely that my parents would find themselves in the same room long enough to discover what I'd threaded together right under their noses.

By the time my dad dropped me off at the Krum house, I could hardly breathe again, or think straight. It was only after Daniel assured me that we were completely alone that I felt safe enough to leave the foyer and follow him into the family room. He must have sensed my uneasiness, because he took me by the hand and led me to the same sofa where we'd been before. I almost wept with relief when he suggested I sit down and finish watching the football game with him on TV.

But I still couldn't loosen up, not even when he pulled me against him and put his arm around my shoulders. It wasn't that I was scared to be alone with him; it was just that being alone with him was so overwhelming. It was like the roller coaster had reached the top of the hill and was holding me over the drop.

And this time when it tilted me over, I feared I wouldn't be able to hold on to the safety bar.

Buying more time, I wriggled out from his arms and walked into the piano room. That's when I went to it, the Steinway baby grand and began to play. It was my way, I guess, of dealing with the mass of emotions clutching my throat. I chose a cheerful sonata, one by Bach, the one Skylar had twirled around to a few weeks before. Daniel's voice was calm. "I love watching you play." Then he asked me to play the one he liked most.

I gave a guess at his favorite, immediately plunging into "Clair de lune." I remembered how I had played the piece when he brought me to his house for the first time and how much it had pleased him.

I couldn't see what he was doing with my back turned, but something told me he wouldn't stay behind me for long. "Ah, that's it," he murmured. Hundreds of rubber bands snapped through my body as I felt more than heard him approach, finally seating himself next to me on the piano bench, with his legs over the other side. I continued to play, and as the crescendo built, his hands moved over me. He drew back my hair and caressed my neck, grazing his lips delicately across my skin.

"I love how you smell," he whispered. His sweet breath warmed my ear. "Your skin is so soft."

As he continued to kiss me, I began to sink into my desire for him. And finally, when the song I was playing became unrecognizable and I no longer could hold a chord, I surrendered and fell into his arms.

In one fluid motion, we moved to the floor, where he lowered his body onto mine. He kissed me, and for the first time I felt free to kiss him back. Free to welcome him into my mouth and move my own hands over his body. Free to finally make him the person who mattered most in my world.

On the floor that afternoon, next to the Steinway baby grand, Daniel and I made love, or at least that's what I convinced myself to believe. He must have known it was my first time, because he was very gentle and asked me over and over as he entered me if I was okay. I didn't really know what to do, so I just lay there. Soon Daniel's breathing slowed and the thrusting came to a gradual end.

Afterward, but for only a few minutes, he held me in his arms. I remember him telling me how we were now as close as two people could be and that we would always have this special bond. To you this might sound like a crock, but to me they were the words that I had been waiting to hear all my life. Even now his words stay with me, sometimes louder, other times softer, but always lingering, holding on to the fragmented pieces of my heart.

"Thank you, Lauren, for giving me this gift," he said, staring into my eyes. "I'll never forget this for the rest of my life. This will be our special secret forever."

But how easily moments can be forgotten, or at least how easily they can fade. My moment with Daniel quickly disintegrated as realized I would have to face his wife after having sex with him in the same room where I'd be soon teaching their daughter how to properly round her fingers over the piano keys. It was this same room where things first had sparked between Daniel and me over an innocent conversation about the beauty of a Steinway baby grand; the same room that I vowed to forever lock in my mind.

Never once did I anticipate how difficult it would be to say hello to Jessica that day or to kneel down to receive Skylar as she wrapped her arms around me. Never once did I think that the beard burn on my face from his unshaven skin could give things away. Never once did I consider that the perfume I wore could have rubbed off on his clothes.

Never once did I think that the guilt would run so deep.

Chapter 25

In the aftermath of sleeping with Daniel, I was slowly falling apart in chunks. If it hadn't been for Daniel calling me from time to time and reassuring me that I had done nothing wrong, I surely would have come completely undone.

And I almost did once or twice as the Christmas season came into full swing. I was a terrible mess. My grades had plummeted and final exams were upon me, but I couldn't study or eat or manage to do anything with a clear head. The guilt over sleeping with Daniel ate at me as much as my longing for him chipped away at my soul. But it wasn't until the Saint Agnes Christmas celebration, the last school Mass before the holiday break that I realized I could no longer carry this burden alone.

It was something Sister Louvois said that stuck with me as she took over the pulpit from Father Glen in Dr. Rainey's absence. I was staring at Daniel's profile as he sat with the rest of the faculty when Sister Louvois went into a passionate spiel about Saint Agnes and how Christmas was a perfect time to remind ourselves to follow her example. In front of a backdrop of brightly lit Christmas trees and a sea of poinsettias, she took us through the virtues of Agnes as Dr. Rainey had done at the start of the semester. She began with *peace* by gesturing to the large crimson banner with the white dove, sharing a short anecdote about how in the face of her accusers, Agnes remained steadfast in her forgiveness, not once lashing out at them for condemning her to an untimely death. Skipping the middle banner, Sister Louvois went on to cover *sacrifice* on her left, reminding us how Agnes had given her life—the ultimate sacrifice—in the name of Jesus Christ. But it was the virtue she saved for the end of her speech—*purity*—that struck a chord with me. For she said it was purity that rounded out the other two. It was purity that made the circle complete.

"Perhaps the most important lesson we can learn from Agnes is her unyielding devotion to Jesus Christ," she preached, gripping the podium with her talonlike fingers. "For even in the face of temptation, Agnes remained pure in mind, body and spirit."

She went on to talk about making wise choices—choices that would bring us closer to holiness in the eyes of God. She spoke of it being a very confusing time in our lives, a time when temptation hides around every corner. She talked of respecting our bodies and keeping our hearts and minds pure by saying no to drugs or sex and other acts of indecency. And she stressed the importance of abstinence and urged us to think twice before allowing the heat of the moment to dictate our decisions.

"The Church does not condone sexual intercourse out of wedlock," she squawked into the microphone, adding that it was her duty and the duty of the faculty members to educate us on Church doctrine. Unlike Dr. Rainey, who was a warm and charismatic speaker, Sister Louvois seemed to look down on us as she spoke. I still see her as a vulture on a treetop, eyeing its prey.

"Sex before marriage, ladies, is a *sin*."

• • •

I didn't make it through the rest of Mass that day or even the remainder of my classes. Before Louvois had finished speaking, I fled the auditorium and went straight to the nurse's office, where I complained of a horrible stomachache. The nurse didn't question me or raise an eyebrow. She even commented that I did look a bit pale and that maybe I should lie down while she tried phoning my mother.

I curled up on the padded table while I heard her talking on the phone. I couldn't tell if it was just terribly drafty in the school that day or if indeed I was coming down with something.

I couldn't stop trembling all over, and it only worsened as the minutes passed.

The nurse had to wake me when my mother arrived. I was still trying to rouse myself from sleep when my mother walked into the small exam room, bringing with her the smell of winter and fresh cigarette smoke. She touched her chin to my forehead and commented that I felt warm and that she needed to get me home and in bed at once.

On the way home I pretended to sleep even though I was awake. I was still so sick from guilt that I was afraid to open my mouth for fear of saying something I might regret. All I wanted was to get in bed and disappear under the covers.

"Do you want me to make you some noodle soup or something?" my mother said as she lingered in my room.

"No, I just want to sleep."

"Okay, honey. I'll come check on you between lessons. Get some rest."

"'Kay."

A few hours later, a thunderous explosion of rock music jarred me awake. I was still struggling against the weight of sleep when Carla barged into my room and started opening and closing my dresser drawers.

"What the hell are you doing?" I sat straight up and fumbled for my glasses. Never did like sleeping in contacts.

"Looking for my earrings," Carla said. The tone of her voice made me shiver.

"What earrings?"

"The ones Shakey gave me."

"What makes you think I have them?"

Carla shot me one of her "fuck you" looks. "Well, for one thing, my makeup has slowly been disappearing, and now I can't find my earrings."

Carla flipped open my jewelry box and rummaged through it. A handful of tiny folded papers hit the carpet. In a sweeping move, Carla scooped one up and pored over it. I saw red.

"Give that to me!" I lunged for it, but she stiff-armed me.

"'Lauren, I can't get you out of my head'?" The way Carla read it made it a question rather than a statement.

"Damn it, give it to me!"

Carla looked amused. "What are you hiding?" she said with a smirk.

"Nothing!" I finally outmuscled her and ripped the note from her hand. I dropped to the floor, frantic to rescue the rest.

"So you actually have a boyfriend?"

"No, I don't have a boyfriend!" I tasted the bitter edge of my words. "And if you fucking say anything to Mom and Dad, then I'll tell them about your late-night romps with Shakey . . . in your bed."

Carla raised an eyebrow as one side of her mouth curled.

"The walls are thinner than you think," I said.

Carla shook her head and smiled. "Wow. Didn't know you had it in ya."

"Have what?"

"The balls to be a bitch."

"Learned it from you."

"Whatever. Let me know if you find my earrings."

As I watched my sister flip her hair and stroll out of my room, I realized that the frayed straps holding me together were about to snap. I had to get this secret out of me before I started bleeding from the mouth. It was eating away at my insides, and if I didn't tell someone soon, I was as good as dead. But that someone couldn't be my mother or my father or my sister, or even anyone on my basketball team. That someone had to be June, simply because I knew she'd never abandon me. No matter what.

That afternoon I called June every ten minutes until she picked up, and then I begged her to come get me. At first she was reluctant, saying that she had a ton of studying to do. But I told her that I didn't care, that this couldn't wait.

"So now, after all these weeks, you actually need me for something more than just a chauffeur?"

I deserved that comment and the coolness in her voice that came along with it.

"You know, ever since you starting going to Saint Agnes, you just dropped me," she continued. "Is our friendship just not good enough for you anymore? Has Saint Agnes turned you into a snob?"

God, I didn't need this. I didn't need to be lectured by June or accused of becoming someone I was not. But I had no choice but to take it because she was the only person I could trust, the only person I knew wouldn't pass judgment on me for my awful secret.

"June, there's an explanation for all of this," I said, trying desperately not to break down. "Please, I'm begging you, come pick me up."

● ● ●

Getting away that afternoon proved more difficult than I had anticipated. Usually my mother was so preoccupied with her piano lessons that she never really gave my comings and goings much attention. That day, though, she seemed uncharacteristically concerned.

"Lauren, I'm not sure I'm comfortable with you going out."

"Mom, I'm feeling better. I slept most of the afternoon and now I've got to study for a final tomorrow, which June said she'd help me with."

It was no secret that June was an absolute brain when it came to academics, so my mom bought this story pretty easily. "I'm just worried about you, baby," she said as I started toward the door. "You haven't been yourself lately."

Of course she was right; I hadn't been myself for a long time. But then again, I didn't know who the real Lauren was anymore. I was living two lives: one for my parents and my teammates, and another for Daniel. If I wasn't careful, the two would converge together to ignite the perfect storm. Lives would be toppled, trusts broken and loyalties destroyed. And me? Well, I'd be left to pick through the rubble and salvage what was left. Then I would know what was real: The good Lauren or the bad Lauren? The innocent Lauren or the guilty? Only one would remain.

As I approached June's car, I felt as if the mask I had been wearing was slowly dissolving. I barely had made it into the passenger seat before tears started spilling from my eyes.

"Lauren, you're scaring me."

And I was scaring myself. As she drove away from my house, my tears turned into uncontrollable sobs that didn't subside until several minutes after she turned into an empty lot by a playground and parked. June didn't press me for answers. She let me cry as much as I needed to, stroking my hair and offering me a T-shirt from the backseat to wipe my face. Several minutes passed before I could get hold of myself.

"I'm having an affair with my coach."

"Get out! Are you shitting me? Because if you are, this isn't very funny."

"Wish I was."

"Is this the guy whose daughter you're giving lessons to?"

"Yeah."

"Does his wife know?"

"No. At least I don't think so."

"Does anyone know?"

"Just you now."

June looked out the window and then turned back to me. "How did it happen?" Her voice was gentle.

"It just did. I went to his house to give Skylar a lesson and …"

"It happened at his house?"

I buried my face in my hands. "I don't know what I'm going to do."

That afternoon in the car, June told me that she wasn't really surprised at my news. That the way I had talked about him, and my sudden interest in makeup and styling my hair, had pretty much given it away. She had a hunch, she said, but now that I had disclosed it all to her, it made perfect sense—my lack of interest in our friendship and in most everything else was directly related to my secret affair with Daniel Krum.

"Did you . . . *do it* with him?"

The muscles around my throat constricted.

"Oh God. You did do it with him."

Not once did she ask me why I had done it or what it was about Daniel that I found so appealing. Not once did she ask me what it felt like to have sex, even though I'm sure she was dying to know. And not once did she make me feel cheap or berate me for the mistakes I had made. Instead she told me that she'd give me her opinion only if I asked for it, and until then she would be there to listen and to lend her support. And she never wavered.

June would later tell me that to save her own conscience, she'd decided early on to emotionally detach herself from the situation, seeing it simply as a challenge that needed a solution rather than a problem that needed fixing. She was methodical in that way, which at times made her come across as cold and uncaring. But she was just who I needed in this situation—someone to push me along and not allow me to fall apart.

"Are you going to keep seeing him?"

I knew absolutely, without a doubt. "Maybe, I guess. I dunno."

Her forehead creased and she looked out the window. And then she asked me a question that only levelheaded June would have thought of. It was a question that turned me inside out, a question that would haunt me for years to come.

"Did he use a condom?"

Chapter 26

It only takes one time . . . one moment in time to set things in motion . . . one millisecond in space to jumpstart a life.

I didn't know how things like this worked, how having sex just one time could result in a pregnancy. June didn't know exactly how it worked either, but being nearly a year older, she probably knew a lot more than me. We decided to figure it out together, starting with the last time I had had a period, but even that proved to be difficult. I couldn't really remember the last time I'd menstruated.

I was a late bloomer, you see, and didn't get my period until I was nearly fourteen years old. If you did the math, that meant I hadn't been menstruating for very long, maybe a year and a half tops. The other problem was that my periods in those days were very unpredictable, as most cycles are at that age.

That has always been fine with me. I hated every time I started to bleed, just as much as I had the first time I awoke to find traces of blood on my sheets. I was constantly paranoid that my bleeding would seep through my clothes for the entire world to see. In fact, I was so devastated when I got my period for the first time that I held off on telling my mother until the toilet paper I had wrapped around my underwear could no longer soak up my blood. She left my room without saying anything and returned with a box of sanitary napkins, or at least that's what she called them. That was the first and the last time we ever spoke of it. I even hid the pads in my room so Carla wouldn't see them because I didn't want her making fun of me. I knew she'd had her period for years by then. Still, I wanted no part of it, the mysterious sisterhood of it all. For some reason I had convinced myself that I would rather die than bleed every month. However, I couldn't stop it from coming . . . couldn't will it to stay buried in the deepest crevices of my womb . . . couldn't prevent it from turning me into a woman.

My father seemed to hate all women. Perhaps that's why I dreaded becoming one. I was the closest thing my father would ever get to a son, a mutant boy child born of his own desperation to fulfill the piece of his manhood that lay empty, his tomboy girl who made every effort to please him by avoiding anything remotely feminine. No bows or ruffles did I wear, and as a child if I'd ever played with Carla's old Barbies, I had done so hidden away in my own closet. Yet the day did come when breast buds sprouted on my chest and hair grew between my legs, and then my period completed the transformation, or better yet, confirmed the gender of my birth. And now, as I desperately waited to bleed, there loomed another witness to my femininity: the possibility of a baby.

"No, June. I'm telling you, there's just no fucking way that could happen!"

"But Lauren—"

"No! I don't want to talk about it anymore, okay?"

We let the line go silent. I had never spoken crossly to June before. Part of me felt badly, while the other part wanted to slap her.

"Look, just hear me out."

"No, June," I snapped. "I've got bigger problems to worry about than something that might not happen for another nine months."

"But if you're—"

"I'm not."

"Lauren, listen to me! If you are pregnant, then you're gonna have to deal with it a lot sooner than that."

"And your point?"

"My point is, if you want to be on the safe side, we need to watch the calendar while we wait for your period to start."

So we waited. We waited through the Christmas holidays. We waited through the start of the new semester. And we waited as Daniel continued to call me, but not as often as he had before. Something seemed to have changed. His voice didn't have the same lift to it as it once had had, and he yawned more and talked less. And the notes in my weekly envelope stopped coming, as did the extra spring in my step. The drug was wearing off; the dose decreasing. I was free-falling back to earth.

June told me several times to just end it; that the whole thing wasn't worth what he and I could both end up losing. But I just couldn't bring myself to do it, not when I truly believed that Daniel and I were meant to be together. In my fifteen-year-old mind, this is what I saw: two people born too far apart, yet we'd still managed to find our way to each other. I clung to this false truth, hoping and praying that somehow, some way, this make-believe romance of ours would work out. I guess I was trying to prove to myself that what we'd done would end up being okay. In my naïve mind, the solution was simple: he could leave his wife. Yes, that was it, I was sure; he could leave her and for three years until I was eighteen we could carry on in secret until it was lawful for us to be together. Yes, that was the solution . . . only if we lived in a dream world.

And then one night something happened that gave me hope. I woke to the sound of rain drumming above me. The phone rang. Carla picked up first, though I quickly came crashing in on the line. I didn't want her to spend any more time speaking with him than she had to. Carla was very curious about "this Sam person," but knowing that I could easily blow the whistle on her sneaking out at night, she knew better than to press me.

"Is Lauren there?"

"Carla, I've got it."

I didn't say anything until I heard Carla disconnect from the line. But I'm sure Daniel could hear me smiling. "Hey."

"Did I wake you?"

"No, the rain did. But I wouldn't have minded if you had, too."

"I need to see you."

The rocks I'd been carrying on my back those last few weeks disintegrated into sand. "You do?"

"Yes. Skylar's got another ear infection and I need to run to the pharmacy to pick up her meds, and I thought ..."

"You thought what?"

"That I could stop by for a few minutes ..."

I shivered at the chance of seeing him, of feeling his arms around me, of his lips pressed against mine.

"Can you get away?" he asked.

"Yeah, I think so," I said, suddenly realizing that he was serious. I thought for a moment. "I can meet you at the end of my street by the stop sign so my parents won't see."

"I'll be there in ten minutes. I'll be in a white Volvo station wagon."

Hurriedly I pulled on my sweatshirt and laced up my sneakers. I didn't have a lot of time to think through my exit strategy. I knew I'd never clear the overgrown bushes outside my bedroom window, so I made a bold move and barged into my sister's room, where I walked straight to her window and threw open the curtains.

"What the hell are you doing?" Carla glared up at me amid the pile of books sprawled across her bed.

I shoved the window open. Rain sprayed in from the outside.

"You can't just waltz in here and—hey! You're letting rain in my room!"

"Would you rather me get rain in your room or tell Dad that I learned to sneak out by watching you?"

"Fuck you, Lauren."

"Thought so." I swung my legs over the window ledge.

"Hey, wait," said Carla.

"What?"

"The gate slams pretty loudly. Make sure you close it gently. It used to squeak, too, but Shakey took care of that."

I gave my sister a smirk and disappeared into the stormy night. Climbing through the window that night, I experienced what it must have felt like to live as my sister did, always teetering on the edge of getting caught and relishing in the thrill of it. I was amazed at how easy it had been for me to sneak around these last few months. It made me wonder if perhaps my sister and I weren't as different as I had once thought, though what I was doing was most likely far worse than anything she had ever done. As I jogged through the rain to the white Volvo wagon parked a few yards from the stop sign, I realized that I was walking the edge of what I knew to be wrong, what I knew to be immoral. And surprisingly, as much as I'd always lived my life by the rules, I was fine with it, if it meant I could have another moment with him, my Daniel.

As I climbed into the warmth of his arms that night, as we reached for each other without words, all the advice that June had given me to end it, to walk away, was lost in his heartbeat.

"You make me crazy." His breath stung my neck. For the first time, I let my greedy little hands explore him, moving over his bare chest, unzipping his pants—

"I missed you so much." He was overcome, breathless. "It's been torture being inches away and not being able to reach out and touch you."

It had been torture for me, too. There had been many times when I thought the cover I'd fastened over my feelings would blow off. We'd been practicing like mad for the district tournament, which would run four to six weeks. He even had told his wife that I wouldn't have time to give lessons to Skylar until after the tournament ended. For me this had come as a relief. The last time I had seen Skylar and her mother was on the day Daniel and I had made love, and to bear that sort of guilt again would have surely have come close to killing me.

But that night in the car with Daniel, I wasn't feeling guilt, I was feeling desire—such a fierce sense of longing that I almost had sex with him again. He awakened something in me, something that perhaps was not meant to come out for another few years, that sexual part of me that still needed to incubate and mature before I could fully protect it from misuse. But through my fifteen-year-old eyes, the ones blinded by my infatuation for Daniel, I only saw my sexual awakening as a gift, a prize given to me for my maturity—and not the criminal mishandling of my innocence that later would nearly rip apart my life.

That night in the car as the rain poured down, Daniel asked me if I'd ever run away with him.

"Do what?" I wanted to hear him say it again.

"If you could, would you run away with me?"

"In a heartbeat."

Chapter 27

To this day, I still wonder why everything happened as it did. I still question whether a deeper meaning exists, one that I still cannot grasp but that I will come to know in time. I cling to this notion, hoping that the affair I had with Daniel Krum wasn't all in vain, and that perhaps the entire situation was orchestrated by God for reasons only He will ever know.

If there was indeed something promising that came out of this tainted romance, I'd have to say it was the way my relationship with my sister improved. After the night I slipped out to meet Daniel, Carla seemed to soften in her dealings with me, treating me for the first time as a human being. This could be simply because I now held something over her that could finish her for good, but I'd like to believe it was something beyond that. For I think when she saw me leaving through her window that night, she began seeing me in a different light, one that had nothing to do with me being Daddy's perfect little angel. Although my rebellion didn't make us instant best friends, it did help us realize that if we were going to survive our household, we had to play on the same team and by the same rules.

Because we were now somewhat cordial to each other, there were many times over the next few weeks when I came close to telling my sister what was going on. Next to June, I knew Carla was the only other person who wouldn't judge me for my actions, but even with this knowledge I couldn't bring myself to do it. Telling even just one other person would make the magnitude of the situation that much more real.

And things were becoming way too real, way too fast. By the second game of the district tournament, strange things were going on with my body. For one thing, I had yet to get my period; for another, I was feeling greener by the day. I was also nodding off during my classes, which wasn't helping my grades any, especially in geometry. I started out the second semester with a 78 on my first test. That earned me a note home from Sister Louvois, stating that if I didn't get my geometry average up to at least an 80, then I could kiss the district tournament goodbye.

Surprisingly, my father wasn't as upset about that note as I had anticipated, probably because I was still the starting point guard. After all, in his mind basketball was the only reason I was attending Saint Agnes. Even if he had exploded, though, I could have handled it. I figured there was nothing worse that could happen to me than getting caught having an affair with my coach or getting pregnant, and up until the tournament I thought I'd managed to avoid both. But after nearly passing out on the basketball court in the middle of game two, I could no longer deny that something was very wrong.

It was midway through the second quarter that a wave of nausea hit me. Beth and I were bringing the ball down the court on an offensive play when I started seeing spots. I gave the signal for time-out and dropped to my knees. Voices echoed in and out, but the only one I was listening for was Daniel's. I didn't care about the game or anyone else, I just wanted him. Only him.

"Lauren, what's wrong?"

Everything disappeared, the players, the crowd, the gym floor. It was just me and Daniel.

"I'm gonna be sick."

He scooped me in his arms and carried me off the court. I buried my face against his neck and felt the familiar burn of his stubble on my skin. I wanted him to keep going, to keep walking right out the door. But when the vomit rose to my throat, I wriggled free of his arms and made it as far as the hallway before I was sick all over the floor. He rubbed my back and told me it was okay. Then he helped me into the locker room, where he sat down next to me on the bench. He stroked my back as I hung over my knees, asked me if I wanted some water and brought me a towel to wipe my face.

"Lauren, we need you in the game . . . *I* need you."

That's all he had to say. "Just give me a few minutes," I said.

"That's my special girl." He squeezed my hand and left me to collect myself, winking at me as he turned the corner.

I walked back out onto the court that night knowing I was in no shape to play. It took me many years and countless therapy sessions to finally realize that Daniel Krum would have won that game at any cost, even at the expense of my own well-being. But to my fifteen-year-old self, to that girl who was only a couple of years removed from training bras and braces, there wasn't anything else I wanted more than for Daniel Krum to need me.

Once I got back in the game, I turned the ball over repeatedly, finally forcing Daniel to take me out toward the end. Our team barely escaped with the win. No one really celebrated when the buzzer sounded, for I think most of my teammates were in shock at how close we had come to losing our chance at a district title so early in the tournament. When none of them asked how I was feeling on the van ride home, it was clear to me how they felt. And I couldn't help taking responsibility for the near-loss, since it was my performance that had left us so vulnerable.

I called June almost the minute I got home and told her about what had happened at the game.

"You threw up?"

"Yeah."

"How are you feeling now?"

"The same. I can't even walk by the kitchen trash without wanting to puke."

"That's not good."

"I know . . . and June, I think you're right. I need to take a test."

She didn't say much to this, except that we'd do it together. The urgency in her voice told me that she didn't believe a pregnancy test would rule out anything, but rather would only confirm what we already knew to be true.

•••

Later that week June picked me up and drove me to a drugstore on the other side of town. We both agreed that if anyone recognized us while we were buying the pregnancy tests, we could find ourselves in a lot of unnecessary trouble. As funny as this might seem, we didn't even know if there was an age restriction on purchasing such products, so we decided the game plan would be for June to do the buying, since she'd turned sixteen during the summer.

"We just need to act like we know what we're doing," she told me on the way there. "Act like we know exactly what we're looking for. Then they won't have any reason to question us."

We finally settled on a Sun Rexall drugstore that had only a handful of cars in the parking lot. Before going in, we guessed that pregnancy tests would be with the pads and tampons in the women's aisle, and that we should start there first.

"Remember," June said as we approached the sliding doors, "we have to act confident."

But I didn't have much confidence left to tap into. We made our way past the aisles, catching side-glances of the category signs hanging above them, and finally ducked down the row labeled Feminine Hygiene. We scanned the rows of product. Only tampons and pads.

"They're not here!"

"Stop freaking out!" June grabbed my hand and led me down the next isle, mumbling under her breath.

"Can I help you girls find something?"

June and I whirled around to find a man as old as our fathers. He had a name tag pinned on his shirt pocket and a belly that hung over the front of his pants.

"No, we've got it, thanks," said June, pulling me toward the pharmacy. I thanked the man and started after her, following the swish of her long black hair as she wove in and out of the aisles. Finally I caught up to her when she came to an abrupt halt, apparently taken by what she saw. There in front of us was an entire section of pregnancy tests located right below the pharmacy counter. A woman and her child stood at the counter, while an older couple waited behind them. Two pharmacy employees bustled around, filling prescriptions.

June took me by the hand and dragged me yet to another aisle, this one filled with variety of cold medicines.

"Take these," she hissed, shoving three boxes of cold remedies into my hands, "and go up to the pharmacy counter and ask them which one's the best."

"What?" I said, not following her.

"Just do it to distract them while I grab a few of the pregnancy tests. Then we'll buy everything at the front of the store, where there aren't as many customers."

Nervously I did as she asked, taking the cold medications to the pharmacist and getting his recommendation on the best one. Being such a tiny person, June easily moved in behind me and did a sweep of the pregnancy tests, which were conveniently stationed by the condoms. I saw this as a clear message that if you found yourself needing one or the other, you'd be forced to endure the disapproving looks of those who happened to be standing by; public scrutiny at its best. And in this God-fearing city, where churches sat on nearly every street corner, you were never far from the steely eye of judgment and the forked tongue of condemnation.

But maybe this was all in my head. Or was it? Scores of overwhelming thoughts and feelings swirled in me during my sophomore year. Was I a bad person? Would I ever get to Heaven? Did Daniel still care? Was there even a baby? The moment these thoughts would creep up from the crevices of my mind, I'd close the door on them, like when you open the pantry and see ants crawling around. You know they're there, but you don't have the energy to clean them all out. So you smile and pretend that everything is okay. Then you take the bag of pregnancy tests from the cashier, fit them under your arm and escape into your best friend's car where nobody can see.

•••

Even though we both had a pretty good feeling I was pregnant, the reality of it hit us hard as we hovered over a dipstick in June's bathroom. I still had two more boxes of tests to take, but I declined to do so once I saw the first thin blue line. It was no use, I told June, for the others would only tell me what I already knew.

We sat in silence for a long time on the cold stone floor of her bathroom, numb to a circumstance neither of us knew how to handle. Here I was fifteen years old and pregnant, without a clue as to what in God's name I was going to do next. I didn't know when the baby would be born or how long I'd be pregnant or even when the right time would be to go see a doctor. Plus I wasn't even sure how the baby would come out of me, how big it would get or worse, since I was so young, whether I'd even survive the birth. But June didn't give me much time to ponder these questions that day. Instead she reminded me about Felicity.

Felicity, a girl at Pope Pius, had gotten herself pregnant during her senior year. When she and her boyfriend voluntarily disclosed the pregnancy to their parents and the school officials, the school decided against expulsion and instead pledged to graduate them as planned. So their sin was forgiven in a sense, but certainly not forgotten—at least not where Felicity was concerned. Over the next few months Felicity continued to attend classes as her belly swelled visibly, forcing her to trade her uniform skirt for maternity clothes and her life for one of constant ridicule.

"Don't you remember how we made fun of her?" June groaned. "Don't you remember how someone wrote 'whore' in permanent marker on her locker?"

I stared blankly at the wall. I did remember, because I had been among those who stared at her in the halls when she passed and whispered secrets behind her back. I, along with the rest of the school, had slowly crucified her each day, making sure she paid for her mistake . . . her unspeakable, dirty sin.

Truth be told, we were no better than Felicity. *I* was no better, now that I found myself staring in disbelief at a dipstick and reeling in the same dimension of shock that she'd slipped through. In fact, I was much worse—worse for having judged her without considering how it might feel to be in her shoes. And now, now I found myself walking in them, surprised at how easily they fit.

June asked me if I would consider confiding in her mother, knowing how liberal she could be with these kinds of things. I was staunchly opposed to the idea, however. I truly did not know how she'd react to the news that her daughter's best friend was on her way to having a baby out of wedlock. But even more, I just couldn't risk my parents finding out. If for some reason Mrs. Hui felt obligated to tell them my secret, I would surely find myself out on the street by my father's hand.

"So tell your mom." June's eyes brightened. "Hey, didn't your Aunt Gina—"

"Yes, she had her son when she wasn't married."

"You could tell her, too!"

"Yeah, and then we could all sit around and celebrate the fact that I was continuing the family tradition."

"What do you mean by that?"

I knew the minute the words left my mouth that June would question them. By "family tradition" I was referring not only to my Aunt Gina's son but also to my sister Carla, whom our mom had conceived out of wedlock. For years now I had managed to keep the latter a secret. For there was something about it that had embarrassed me . . . something that for years had made me feel above it . . . something in my twisted mind that had convinced me that if it was to happen again, Carla would be the likely candidate. After all, she was the one who had been the love child, and with her wild behavior it seemed only fitting for something like this to cast its shadow on her. But instead it had come upon me, even though for most of my life I had been the good girl, the good sister who always did everything right.

Leaving June's house that day, I got the sinking feeling that I was no closer to finding a solution to my problem than before I confirmed the pregnancy. And that's how I regarded it now—as a problem. I felt no attachment or loving feelings for any child that might be growing inside me, and if it had not been for the test results staring me in the face, I might not have acknowledged its existence at all. In fact, I tried not to even think about it for the rest of the weekend; if I allowed myself to linger on it even for a moment, the mass of hysteria slowly building in my gut would roll up into my throat and explode out of me. If it weren't for June calling me on Sunday night, I might have ignored it all the way up to the time of delivery.

"I've thought of a couple more options for you," she said, trying to sound hopeful.

"What?" I was not in a mood to discuss what I considered to be the end of my life.

"Have you thought about telling Daniel?"

My mouth went dry. "No. I'm not going to do that."

"But he's the father, Lauren! He might just be the person who could help you most."

Or the least.

"If you were a thirty-five-year-old man with a wife and kid, would you really jump at the chance of helping your pregnant fifteen-year-old girlfriend?"

"You consider yourself his *girlfriend*?"

I don't really remember hanging up on June, but she later said that by doing it, I got the message across to her that I no longer wanted to discuss my relationship with Daniel Krum. I don't think it was June whom I was really mad at; I was mostly angry with myself and June just happened to be in the line of fire at the time. Nevertheless, she went on to apologize for upsetting me, but also said that if I was really going to get through this, I'd have to face it all now, as painful as it might be, before time ran out. And what I found myself thinking was what did Daniel have to worry about? Winning the district title? Like it was all butterflies and flowers for him now.

June's voice broke into my thoughts. "I pulled out some of Saul's anatomy books, and you could be close to your second trimester," she said, flipping pages on the other end of the line. "Your window of options is closing."

Although I had no idea what this talk of trimesters meant, her mention of Saul's name caught my attention. Saul, you see, was June's twenty-four-year-old brother, who had watched me grow up right alongside his sister. Like June, he was the perfect combination of his parents; he had his father's brains and his mother's French charm. And he was somewhat of a prodigy, having graduated from high school at sixteen and college at twenty. At sixteen, I was thinking, my life would look quite different, especially if I was holding the bastard child of Daniel Krum in my arms.

"Lauren! Did you hear what I said?"

"Whah? No, what did you say?"

"I said, you don't have to keep the baby."

Chapter 28

I wasn't sure if I had heard June right.

"Wait, did you just say that I don't have to keep the baby?"

"Yes."

"What, like, give it up for adoption?"

"No." I could almost hear June calculating her next words. "What I mean is, you could have an abortion."

This couldn't be happening. I was only fifteen. This was someone else's horror story. Abortions were for prostitutes and people who lived on the south side of Dallas, where housing projects were more common than a white person walking down the street in broad daylight. Not for a girl who lived in the northeast part of the city, went to private school and was the star of her basketball team.

Maybe I should have befriended the pro-lifers who passed out flyers after church. Maybe I should have emptied my pockets into the collection basket at Mass to help protect the unborn. Or maybe I should have taken a closer look at the billboard on Highway 75, the one with a photo of the Blessed Virgin Mary that says "Pregnant? Need Help?" But did that message also come with a guarantee that my father wouldn't kill me, and that society wouldn't cast on me the scarlet letter "A"?

June was very convincing. She said that if I chose to keep the child, there would be no conceivable way to hide the pregnancy, which meant that the world would eventually have to find out. She told me that a baby would drain all chances of me having a shot at a real future; and unless I wanted to be trapped with a reminder of Daniel Krum for the rest of my life, then I had better give this option some serious thought and consideration.

"I could call Saul," she said finally. "He might know about these things. Maybe he could help us."

I'll be very honest with you. Despite all my reservations about an abortion, by the end of our conversation I could finally get in a full breath of air. I just couldn't see myself going down the same path as my mom or my Aunt Gina, and if there was a way, I'd avoid it altogether. To me they were trapped—trapped in a life with no options. For years I had witnessed how miserable my mom was, and even though Aunt Gina always put on a happy face, I knew her life had had its share of struggles; it had been difficult for her just to make ends meet. And I just couldn't imagine going through the same thing.

What my immature mind failed to recognize, however, was that perhaps getting pregnant wasn't necessarily the main reason that the lives of my mother and aunt had turned out the way they had. Baby or no baby, they could have easily ended up taking the same course, with my mom still marrying my father and Aunt Gina still jumping from boyfriend to boyfriend and struggling for every dollar she made. Could we really break this down to something as simple as a choice? Like my decision to let Daniel kiss me that day in his home? But despite how the cards could have fallen, both my mother and Aunt Gina had one thing in their favor that I did not: age. They were young, but there's a big difference between getting pregnant in your twenties and having a baby when you're considered barely out of childhood yourself.

With this in mind, I reluctantly allowed June to call her brother and confide in him what was going on. It saddened me that Saul would have to find out about my pregnancy. I had always looked up to him and regarded him as the closest thing to having a brother of my own, and the thought of him thinking less of me was just too heavy to bear. I knew, though, that I had no choice but to trust him, especially if I wanted any chance of making it through this mess.

•••

It didn't take long for June to make contact with her brother, and just as we had expected, my situation proved disturbing to him. In fact, he made it clear that before he would give her any information, he wanted to meet with us in person.

This upset me. I didn't want to have to talk to anyone, even if the person was June's brother. I suppose I had hoped that she would just get the information from him and it would be done.

"I don't need to be lectured, June!" I told her in a fit of frustration. "I already know what I did was horrible . . . I don't need anyone reminding me of that."

"He doesn't want to lecture you, Lauren. He's just concerned. This isn't something you can make go away that easy."

Well, no shit. As if I didn't already clearly understand the seriousness of the situation! Being so sick gave me a constant reminder of what was going on with my body, or in other words, how securely dug in this child was becoming by the day. No matter how much I drove myself to the ground during the tournament games, or how much I threw up, the kid still managed to hang on. The more the baby grew, the more my future would be rewritten—a future that hadn't really even begun. It would be a future that belonged to no one really—not to me, not to the married man who didn't know about our baby, and not even to the baby, the one I knew now I couldn't keep.

My future, my story would not be altered. I would unfetter the chains that bound me.

Chapter 29

Saul, as it turned out, was easy to confide in. When June and I arrived at his apartment, he greeted me like he always had, but in a manner that was much more somber and serious than I had remembered.

Seeing Saul for the first time in his own place made him seem so grown-up. He still had that boyish look about him, with his jet-black hair buzzed to the scalp, and that signature smile he shared with his dad. But something about him had matured, and that night as I sat across from him in the space of his own living room, a Rolodex of memories flipped through my mind, taking me back to a time when the only thing we had to worry about was our next chance to play outside.

Growing up, that's where June and I differed; she seemed content to play with her dolls, but I was always looking for an opportunity to join in a game of basketball with Saul and his friends. He never really minded when I came out to play, probably because when I did manage to sneak away from June and her Barbies, I was never intimidated to play against the older boys. Or maybe they just went easy on me. Whatever it was, I think Saul always respected my effort in sports, seeing me perhaps as the adopted tomboy sister. Don't get me wrong, he loved his sister, but June was 100 percent girl. I, on the other hand, hung somewhere in between. Ironic how I came crashing into womanhood so much sooner.

Memories of our childhood together quickly faded as Saul shifted in his chair to face me, resting his forearms on his knees and then leaning back again as if trying to get comfortable. I sensed the situation itself was making him tense. Our interactions had never gone beyond shooting the shit, and yet here we were about to discuss my pregnancy. I sat there feeling ashamed that I had put Saul in such a position, but even more, I felt ashamed of what he must think of me now that I was no longer a virgin. I could only dare to imagine the image of me this conjured in his mind. Did he see me there in the living room, or through me to my silhouette humping and grinding a faceless man, giving up my body like some goddamned whore?

"June tells me you're in some trouble," he said finally, taking a swig from his Coke and lowering it back on the coffee table. "Do you know how far along you are?"

"No." I looked away and then back again.

"We were hoping you could help us with that," June said.

Saul's eyes darted to his sister and then back to me without the slightest movement of his body. As if buying time, he took another swallow of Coke before asking his next question.

"Do you know the date of your last period, then?"

"Saul, I told you on the phone that she doesn't know!" snapped June.

"June, I'm talking to Lauren—not you!"

June folded her arms and leaned back against the sofa in a huff.

"She's right. I don't know exactly—maybe over the summer sometime?"

"When did you start having sex?"

I wrung my hands together. "It was only one time . . . the first week in December."

"Did he force you?"

"What do you mean?"

June interrupted before he could answer. "Saul, you promised you wouldn't ask a lot of questions!"

Saul shot his sister a look. "June, stay out of this!" Then, turning back to me: "Lauren, the thing that happened to you—"

June jumped up. "Saul, this wasn't our deal!"

"June, it's okay," I said. She looked at me as if I were crazy and sat back down. I turned to answer Saul, although I wasn't sure where he was going with this.

"No, he didn't force me. I did it willingly."

Saul shifted his weight forward and rested his elbows on his knees. "Okay. But did you know that given your age, in a court of law this would be considered statutory rape?"

"What's that mean?"

"It means that in the eyes of the law, you're below the age to legally consent to having sex."

"Am I in trouble?"

Saul shook his head. "Lauren, no, no, you're not in trouble! This guy raped you."

The synapses in my brain misfired. I had thought rape was when a stranger grabbed you in a dark alley, beat up your face and then forced himself between your legs. My thoughts broke off and that's when I realized someone was shaking me.

"Lauren?" I looked at June. It took me a half second to register her face. "Are you okay?"

But Saul didn't give me time to respond. "Lauren, I know this is a lot. But I think you need to consider turning this guy in."

I don't remember standing up or pacing around, because I was much too angry to keep track of my movements or the volume of my voice. "No! I'm not gonna do that!"

I felt June's hand curl around my forearm. "Lauren, it's okay," she said.

I ripped my arm out of her hand. "No, it's not okay! He did not rape me!"

That was the first time I'd ever really shouted at June, and the shock on her face told me everything I needed to know. I was slowly losing it, just like my dad.

"Lauren, it's okay." Saul waved me back over to the sofa. "I'm trying to help you."

"By telling me that I was raped?"

Saul shook his head at me. "Look, I'm not going to argue with you about this. Do you want my help or not?"

Saul was my one and only chance of getting out of this mess. "Yes."

"Then here's the deal." Saul leaned forward. "There is someone I know at the hospital—a doctor—who is rumored to take on things like this, patients like you. Rape victims."

I set my jaw. "I told you I'm not a rape victim."

"Then this doctor won't give you an abortion."

"Then I'll go to someone else."

"Lauren, I don't think you understand," he said gently. "You need parental consent because you're a minor."

Parental consent. I'd had no idea. No idea that in order to end a pregnancy, you had to get permission—from your parents. Were there really parents who did that? Helped their daughters have abortions? I knew that would never happen at my house. My father, I was sure, would much rather see me dead than admit his younger daughter was carrying the bastard child of a man he'd vote for coach of the year.

"So you're saying that in order to get this doctor to do this for me, I have to lie and say that I was raped?"

"Call it what you want, but yes, that's what I'm saying."

June and I left Saul's apartment that day in silence. Saul's insistence that Daniel Krum had raped me had I'm sure made her think. But if he had indeed swayed her, she didn't let on, and for that I was thankful. I wasn't in the mood for another lecture like the one Saul had given me, even if it was done with good intentions.

For years afterward I refused to believe that Daniel Krum had raped me—manipulated me perhaps, but not raped. I could have stopped him, I could have told him no. I could have placed my hand on his and gently guided it out from under my shirt. I could have shoved him off me, buttoned my jeans and left. But I didn't. I didn't do any of this. Not even after we had sex. Not during the phone calls or the longing, lonely days. Because the truth to all this, the truth that still drives me so absolutely crazy, is that I just wanted him to hold me, just wanted him to love me, just wanted him to make me his. And even if I had understood all the consequences of our affair, I think the plot of my story would've still unfolded in the same way.

The week dragged on as I waited for June to call with news from her brother. The plan was for Saul to set things in motion by making contact with the doctor. How he was going to do this I wasn't sure, but he had made it seem all very secretive, warning both June and me not to breathe a word.

It's hard to face the world when you're carrying such a heavy secret. No matter how hard you try to go on with your daily life, it weighs on you like bricks in your backpack, causing you to do everything a half step slower and slightly off course. And for me there wasn't just one secret but three: my affair with Daniel Krum, the pregnancy and now my pending abortion. I was barely holding on, but as June pointed out, there really wasn't anything more that could be added to the list.

Unless, of course, your name happens to be Jessica Krum.

Chapter 30

Never did I imagine that a woman I hardly knew would end up holding the fate of my future in her hands. Never did I think that Jessica Krum would find out about my affair with her husband. And never did I consider that she would be so cruel—so full of hate.

But then again, I deserved it, or at least I thought I did until just a few years ago. Some nights, when I hear that song by Depeche Mode or see a girl with an older man, I start tearing into myself again, wondering, doubting. Sometimes hating. But I try not to do that anymore. The real truth is—well, it's not so clear. All I know is that I never saw it coming.

And I never saw Jessica coming, that's for sure. If I hadn't caught the scent of her perfume as I turned the corner on my way to practice that day, I might have run smack-dab into her, knocking both her and Skylar over as they stood glued together against the brick wall. They were both wearing matching red coats, black hats and gloves, looking pretty as pretty can be with their rosy cheeks and noses seared from the cold. Skylar immediately ran over and wrapped her arms around me, only to have Jessica abruptly pull her away. Still wearing her beauty pageant smile, Jessica gently told her daughter to go find her daddy in the gym so she and Miss Lauren could have a chat.

A tremendous sense of dread came over me as I watched the curly-haired little girl bound away. Without Skylar there to stand between us, Jessica could do to me as she pleased, and it didn't take a genius to figure out that this, her showing up to find me at school, was by no means a social call.

After her daughter was well out of earshot, Jessica turned to me. Since she was still smiling sweetly, I clung to the hope that perhaps I had read her wrong and that really she was here to discuss starting up Skylar's lessons again.

"Lauren, could we have a word, please?" Her voice was glass—sharp, cut glass—and the smile she wore wasn't genuine, but clearly a cover-up for whatever was brewing behind it.

Knowing full well that she hadn't intended it as a question, I nodded and shuffled behind her as she turned and strode toward the parking lot. The heels of her boots clicked on the ground as she moved along the pavement, never once losing her balance despite the icy wind whipping at our backs. For someone so petite, she walked surprisingly fast, so fast I could barely keep up with her.

When she motioned for me to get in the white Volvo station wagon, the same one Daniel had driven the night he came to see me, I trembled a little. And it wasn't because I'd forgotten to wear my winter coat. He and I had done stuff . . . right inside this white Volvo wagon, and now we weren't the only ones who knew.

She said a lot of things to me, but I was too numb to hear much of it. I kind of tuned out, at least until she pulled out sheets of paper and threw them in my lap. It didn't take me long to figure out what they were.

They were copies, you see. Oh God, she had copies of his notes to me. "I've got to see you, Lauren . . . You're all I think about, Lauren . . . I'll try calling you tonight, Lauren . . . You're driving me crazy, Lauren." And so on and so on. I had no way of disproving them. No way of rendering them false. No way of explaining how and why they had all come to be.

I didn't even bother trying to defend myself, for the evidence was there in black and white. So I sat there deflated. I couldn't move or speak or even breathe. And I couldn't bear to be the person I was anymore. I hated myself, probably more than even Jessica Krum hated me, and I hated that I hadn't been strong enough to prevent all of this from spiraling so far out of control.

She finally stopped her yelling and turned back into the model of refinement she had been only moments before. Without another glance at me, she pulled down the visor, checked her makeup in the mirror and quietly told me to get the hell out of her car and never to show my face around her again. And how could I blame her? I'd slept with her Daniel. He belonged to her and not me. I felt like a whore and a thief.

I still had the letters in my lap, so I pulled them together as best I could, got out of the car and staggered into the building. It was only when I was dialing June's number on the pay phone outside the cafeteria that I started to break down. By the time June answered her phone, tears were flooding my eyes and pouring down my face. I didn't know what to do; I didn't know where to turn. But what I did know was that I couldn't go to basketball practice and face Daniel, not after what had just occurred.

June told me to stay put; she would get there as fast as she could. So with the papers stuffed in my backpack, I huddled on the curb trying to collect myself, praying to God to make the day end. It didn't end, though. What I remember next is wondering if He had decided to take the afternoon off or ignore my prayer altogether, because I heard the pitchy voice of Sister Louvois calling out to me from the top of the steps.

"Lauren Muchmore, why aren't you at practice?"

"I'm not feeling well," I said, jumping to attention. "I'm waiting for my sister to pick me up."

She craned her neck for a better look. "What seems to be your ailment?"

"My stomach—it's been hurting for most of the day."

"And whom did you say you were waiting for?"

"My sister, Carla. She's coming to get me."

"Yes, I believe I met her at your home last year." She paused. "Does Coach Krum know that you are ill?"

"I guess I forgot to tell him."

"So the fact that he was expecting you at practice just slipped your mind?"

Right as Sister Louvois looked as if she was going to lay into me, June pulled up. And of course she got out and waved at me. "Are you ready?" she said.

A satisfied expression spread across Sister Louvois's face. She had caught me in a lie and was obviously thrilled about it.

"Your sister has changed a bit since the last time I saw her," she said, eyeing June. "Do you want to tell me what's really going on?"

I backpedaled, telling the nun that what I had meant to say was that my friend June was picking me up and not my sister. But Louvois didn't buy my story—or my suspicious behavior— and announced that my friend would have to wait while I accompanied her to the gym, where we'd clear the matter up with Coach Krum.

Damn that Sister Louvois . . . damn her right down to her beak of a nose.

The next thing I knew, she was marching me across the lawn toward the gym. My teammates gawked when we barged in. Daniel blew the whistle and trotted over like a finely-tuned athlete.

"Lauren, we've been worried about you."

He looked me in the eyes and then turned to Sister Louvois. An insolent smile broke across one side of her face.

"I found her on the curb, waiting for her ride."

"I'm not feeling well," I said.

"But I told her that she should have let you know first before she decided just to skip practice," Sister Louvois said.

"If she sick, she's sick." He shrugged. "I need my players healthy."

"But aren't you bothered that she didn't tell you?"

"Well, sure I am, but Lauren's one of my best—I can trust her."

When he said, "I can trust her," he looked right at me. Then he gave me a grin—one of his special grins reserved for me.

"Well, if I were you, I'd give her detention. But like you said, she's your player and you can do with her as you wish."

If she only knew.

Chapter 31

The way I saw it, Daniel owed me one, and getting me out of the crosshairs of Sister Louvois was a good start. As for the rest of it, I hadn't really thought about what else he could do; and looking back now, I still don't really know. Even then, despite my fantasies, I didn't really expect him to run away with me and raise our child. The whole idea was scary to me. I didn't know how to be a mom yet. I mean, who does at fifteen? I didn't know what I wanted. I didn't know what I was doing. I was a wreck.

Of course, I can see that it wasn't about what I should or shouldn't have done. Now I know that it was really only about what *he* should or shouldn't have done. After all, he was the adult, and I was just fifteen.

Hindsight's a wonderful thing when it's used properly.

At the time, though, I was more concerned with trying to figure out how Daniel's notes had come into his wife's hands. That, and the question of what Jessica planned to do with them, consumed me.

The answer finally hit me late one night that it was Beth, and probably her sidekick Emerson, who'd had something to do with it. I'd moved the notes to my gym locker to hide them from Carla, thinking they'd be safe there. The whole thing seems stupid now. But as my therapist likes to remind me, we were just girls, dealing with an adult situation that we shouldn't have been dealing with in the first place. In retrospect, I also don't think

Beth and Emerson really meant to be that cruel. I'd like to say that I've forgiven myself like I've forgiven them. But I'm still working on that.

I look back on this now and I think about forgiveness, but I wasn't thinking about it then. I was thinking, actually about another way out, even though I knew all bets would be off if I killed myself. I quietly thought about it, contemplating the ways in which I'd do it and who I'd like most to discover my body. It sounds gruesome and even petulant, but I settled on my dad and Daniel Krum. It would give them exactly what they deserved—or so I was thinking. I daydreamed through the scenarios and even went as far as imagining my own funeral. But still I couldn't do it, and not because I didn't have the guts to pull it off. I couldn't do it simply because of what I'd been taught—that by taking your own life, you commit a mortal sin, damning your soul to hell for eternity.

I'm relieved now, looking back, but at the time I thought I was just being selfish in deciding not to end it all.

Chapter 32

During the course of my affair with Daniel Krum, there were many times that the image of Saint Agnes haunted me, reminding me how she represented everything I was not.

There was one particular likeness of Agnes that I found most captivating—a life-size statue displayed in the entryway of the school. It greeted me every morning as I entered the double doors, though sometimes the scores of girls speeding through blocked my full view of it, giving me only a glimpse of her cloak-covered head.

Except for the sword she held firmly in her hand, she looked like a fair young maiden, all draped in emerald green and gently cradling a lamb. She seemed to be peering up at the sky in a fit of passion, her eyes transfixed in a hypnotic sort of way, but still heavy with grief and desperation. Blood dripped from the tip of the sword, spilling down her wrist and onto the ground. A palm leaf lay at her feet.

I could go on all day about what this symbolized, about how the lamb represented her virginity and the blood-drenched sword signified how far she had gone to protect it. Of course that was only my interpretation, but it was one that seemed to go along with her role, as Sister Louvois had explained, as protectress of bodily purity.

I came to resent this rendering of Agnes not for what it

stood for, but for how it made me feel. It made me feel dirty and sinful, almost unworthy of being in its presence at all. During those dark days when my life seemed to be at its worst, I would hold my breath and keep my eyes focused on the crimson carpet as I sneaked past it, willing myself not to look and damning myself for not being more like her.

One morning, and it ended up being an important morning, I avoided the statue entirely, asking June to drop me off at the back of the school near the cafeteria instead. I was terrified as it was at what would be happening to me that day, and I didn't need the reminder of what I was about to do.

"Do you want me to pick you up right here when I come back?"

Oh, sweet June. She was risking her skin to save my own. My plan was to convince the school nurse that I wasn't feeling well and tell her that I needed to call my mom. Even now I remember standing in the front office and picking up the receiver, hearing the buzz of the dial tone and then punching random numbers as I pretended to phone my mother. I waited a few moments and began a mock conversation with her, saying that I had a terrible stomachache and that I needed to be picked up right away. The nurse glanced up from her desk a couple times and eyed me momentarily, but the pile of paperwork in front of her soon won her attention, allowing me to finish my mock dialogue without incident. Impulsively I said the words "I love you" at the end, while the standard recording "If you would like to make a call, please hang up and try again" echoed on the line.

I'm not sure why I said this, for this kind of affection was never shared in my family. If the nurse had known me better, she could have picked up on this as the obvious clue that my conversation had been a fake.

Nonetheless I made it out of there, exiting the school on the east side by the junior parking lot. My locker was located in this same wing, which made it easy for me to load my backpack and slip through the doors. I ran around the south end of the building, ducking below the rim of classroom windows until I came upon a set of double doors, which just so happened to be swinging open at the precise moment I was walking by.

"Lauren?"

I guess if a teacher was going to catch me, it was best that the teacher be Daniel Krum. It's not like he would've turned me in, for he had lost that authority months before on the day he leaned down and kissed me.

"Are you all right?"

Was I all right—how could he ask me that? Of course I wasn't all right. In fact, I was barely hanging on.

"I'm not feeling well," I said, fighting my emotions.

There was a moment as I looked into his eyes that I thought maybe he knew, that maybe through mental telepathy he had figured out the secret I was carrying for both of us. I wanted so badly to take him by the hands and tell him what was going on. I wanted so badly to tell him that I needed his help, and that I was scared. So scared.

"I'm sorry to hear that. Is there anything I can do?"

How was I supposed to answer that? If June had been whispering in my ear, she would have insisted I tell him what I was about to do. She'd have told me to ask for help, or at least to ask him to pay for it. But that wasn't my way. I guess you could say I didn't want to impose—which is so warped if you think about it, especially because I was carrying his child.

His question hung in the air. *Is there anything I can do?* I could think of a number of things, none of which I was able to force from my mouth. If I hadn't been rendered speechless, I would have told him how much I needed him, how scared I was, how guilty I felt. I'd have told him how much I missed him and how when we were alone, he always made me feel like I was floating on a cloud. He made me feel special. He made me feel loved.

But none of that mattered then, none of it could have or would have made a bit of difference. I started to thank him, mumbling something about missing practice. And just when he was thanking me for letting him know, June pulled up and I waved to him, looking back over my shoulder once.

"Who was that?" asked June, glancing back in his direction as she drove away.

My first instinct was to tell her it was him. Daniel Krum, the man I had lost everything to . . . the man to whom I had lost my way. But for some reason I just couldn't bring myself to do it.

"Just a teacher," I said, watching his reflection in the side view mirror. "Just a teacher I know."

Chapter 33

The details of how I got on that table aren't really important. The fact is I was lying in that clinic, in that operating room, waiting for it to be over. And it's not an easy thing to talk about even now. There I was on that table, and a nurse was sticking an IV in the top of my hand, attempting several times to find a vein. On my other arm, a second nurse took my blood pressure, which I heard her say was a little high. And then they left me shivering on the table, and told me that the doctor would be in to see me shortly, and in the meantime I should close my eyes and relax. But there was no possible way for me to relax, for I was shaking uncontrollably now, and to this day I don't know if it was the result of the arctic temperature in the room or because of the fear running through my body. As I lay there alone in the stark white exam room, tears flooded my eyes at the realization of what I was about to face.

And then my mind drifted and I began to think about Agnes. I began to think about how she must have felt being put to death at such a young age, how fear must have consumed her during those final moments of her life. I know you can't compare the two, but somehow I drew strength knowing that she might have encountered the same fear . . . fear of desolation, of facing the end, of not knowing what lay beyond.

As I pondered this, I found myself praying to her and asking her to stand there next to me as I went under the knife.

Call it a coincidence, but toward the end of my prayer, a woman in scrubs strode in, casting a calming aura about the room.

"Hi, I'm Dr. Williams. You must be Lauren."

She shook my hand firmly and smiled as she looked me over. She asked me if I was cold, and when I said yes, she left my bedside, leaned her head out the door and like a drill sergeant, barked at one of the nurses, "Do patients have to get frostbite around here to get a warm blanket?"

I was in awe of her, not only because she made people jump at the snap of her fingers but because this doctor standing before me and tucking the ends of a blanket on either side of my body was miraculously, I thought, a woman. Call this a product of growing up in a man's world, but it never occurred to me that "C.B. Williams, MD" would turn out to be a female, and such a confident one at that. As nurses raced around the room, Dr. Williams seemed suspended in slow motion, sweeping her hair back behind her ear and studying my chart. "Can you give us a minute," she said, peering up from her reading glasses at the nurses bustling around her. Like trained dogs, they all dropped what they were doing and scurried out the door, leaving the two of us alone.

"Lauren," she said, pulling a stool over to the side of my bed. "Let me cut right to the chase. I don't make it a habit to help girls your age."

"Thank you," I said.

"I don't need your thanks—I just want you to consider turning in the person who did this to you. Okay?"

"All right," I said, realizing that my nails were digging into my palms.

"Okay, then. Let's get on with it, shall we?"

The memory of what happened next is still painful. When it flows over me, I go back into my body, fifteen and little again. I remember fearing that my heart would beat out of my chest as they positioned my legs in the cold metal stirrups and told me to scoot my bare bottom as close to the edge of the table as possible. At one point I think I started hyperventilating, and then a nurse placed a mask over my nose and mouth. "Lauren, this will help you relax," she said. "It'll make you feel like you're floating." Soon after, the cramping came on like a tidal wave and I remember asking if I was going to die. The nurse told me it would be over soon, but the pain just kept coming and coming, as if someone was gutting me like a fish. And finally, when I could barely hold back from screaming, the pain slowly lifted, taking me back to the place where I was floating again, edging me away from what I was certain was the threshold of hell.

I never saw Dr. Williams again after that day, even though the nurses told me I needed to come back in a week for a post-op exam. I'm sure you'd agree I took a chance by not following through on their instructions, especially not knowing if the procedure had caused any long-term damage to my ability to have children, something I might never know. I guess at the time I felt I just needed to move on with my life and forget what had happened. But the truth, and I see it now, is that if I had returned for that post-op appointment, I would have found it difficult to face Dr. Williams again, knowing that I had no intention of ever turning in the person who in her words "did this to me."

I'm sorry, Dr. Williams. Really, I am.

Chapter 34

If you ask me, God has a sick and twisted sense of humor.

It had been three weeks or so since the abortion, and life as I had once known it was gradually getting back to normal. But my mind was still in shambles. I had dreamed of her, the baby, a little girl. I dreamed that I was holding her in my arms. Her eyes were blue; her skin, a rosy pink.

Somehow I managed to pick myself up and continue where I had left off, playing the role of the diligent Saint Agnes student and gifted point guard and leading my team to a district title only a few days after I had done away with Daniel Krum's child.

But I saw the world differently now—a world that had been spoiled by all the lies and deception that had marked my second high school year. It was hard for me to look forward to the future and recognize any good that it might bring, especially when I was faced with two more years of Daniel Krum as my basketball coach and the possibility of him becoming my chemistry teacher the following term. Of course June and I had discussed the prospect of my switching schools again and going back to Pope Pius. But I didn't see how I'd convince my father that this was a good idea, much less get up the nerve to even broach the subject in the first place.

Seeing no other option, I became resigned to the fact that for the next two years, I'd be forced to live with a daily reminder of my sins and to carry out my penance alongside the very man who had made me so weak. I considered this to be God's ultimate test of my self-reformation, the ultimate test of whether I could resist temptation or not.

For I was sure He was already testing me as Daniel readied us for the state tournament, testing me when Daniel's hand would just so happen to graze my arm, testing me as I inhaled the scent of his aftershave as he passed me in the halls, testing me at night when I secretly longed to talk to him, testing me in my dreams, in my thoughts and in my heart. Testing . . . testing . . . testing . . . never ceasing in His attempts to trip me up.

I was determined to prove God wrong, and wipe out my feelings for Daniel Krum forever. I remember even telling June that it seemed to be getting easier to be around him, that standing next to him no longer caused my knees to knock or my heart to skip. With each new day I was actually willing myself to get over him, and by the start of the state tournament, I was walking through the halls of Saint Agnes with a renewed sense of purpose and a feeling of confidence that could have propelled me to the moon. I was beating it; beating the temptation to love him again and overcoming the all-consuming feeling to let what had happened get the best of me.

But apparently God wasn't quite done with me yet. He needed one last laugh at my expense . . . one last jab to remind me of my disobedience.

It was toward the end of my history class when Sister Louvois slipped into the classroom and whispered something in my teacher's ear. My teacher nodded and then found my eyes. That's when the bomb went off in my chest.

"Lauren, will you please accompany Sister Louvois to her office?"

While I was getting a head start on my reading, Sister Louvois had slipped into the classroom and made her way to the front of the class without my noticing. I rose and followed her, but she sped right through the door ahead of me, letting it swing closed behind her so that I had to stop it with my forearm before it hit me in the face. She walked several strides in front of me along the crimson carpet. I followed her past the statue of Saint Agnes to the administration area and then around the corner to her office, where she slammed the door behind me the moment I crossed its threshold.

"Sit."

I remember how my neck prickled with heat as she opened a file drawer on the underside of her desk and pulled out a manila legal-size envelope. Next thing I knew she had hurled it into my lap, where I sat there staring at it, waiting for her to tell me what to do next.

"Well, by all means, open it."

I turned it over and studied the name on it: "Sister Louvois." I fumbled with the latch, opened the flap and slowly pulled out a thin stack of papers.

I recognized them right away. They were Daniel's letters, and now Sister Louvois had a set of her own.

Several moments passed before she spoke again, during which time I'm sure she contemplated expelling me on the spot or some other form of punishment equal in severity. Whatever she was thinking, she never stopped glaring at me, her face a pressure cooker ready to burst. And finally it did.

"How long has this been going on!" she said, slamming her hand flat on her desk. "Look at me, girl, when I'm talking to you!"

"Sister Louvois, it's not what you think!"

"Don't lie to me, girl!" she spat, pointing her finger at me. "Do you take me to be some kind of fool?"

"No!" I said, feeling defenseless. "No, Sister, I don't. Please, let me—"

"Are you still having relations with him?"

"No!"

"Are you sleeping with him?"

"No!"

Visibly angered, the nun rose and began pacing around the room, her eyes bitter, her brow furrowed. At one point she whispered to herself, clutching her hands together in prayer and speaking in a tongue she must have meant only for God. After a minute or so of this, she turned to me and said abruptly, "Get out of my office and go wait outside. And don't do *anything* until I say you can."

Outside her door I sat motionless, not wanting to cause any more trouble than what was already coming to me. Her voice filtered through the wall in low tones and murmurs. She was on the phone, and I knew exactly who was on the other line.

My parents.

There would be no way now to prevent them from finding out. I was a sitting duck, doomed in a worse way possible. Sister Louvois didn't know my father. She didn't know how angry he could become. She didn't know the depth of his rage.

I was certain that by calling my parents Sister Louvois had just ordered my death sentence—whether she realized it or not. And if a death sentence was indeed what God had coming to me, then my father would be the first in line to carry it out. *God giveth, God taketh away.*

The door to Sister Louvois's office swung open, breaking me away from my thoughts. With one hand on her hip she ordered me back inside, where I was to wait until she returned.

"Back inside, and don't touch anything," she said, waving her finger at me. "If you do, I'll know."

This time there would be no escape.

Chapter 35

When an hour or so later I heard the jingle of keys outside the office door, it was my mother who entered the room first, a frightened and confused look on her face. Sister Louvois asked politely if she minded waiting with me until my father arrived, at which time she would explain the nature of this inconvenience.

"Of course," my mother said, clearly eager to oblige. "I've cancelled the rest of my lessons for the day, so that won't be a problem."

With that, Sister Louvois left us alone, my mother clutching her bag as if it were a life vest. I just stared at her. I had no idea what to say to this woman who had given me birth.

"Lauren—"

"Mom, he's going to kill me."

"Your father's going to be here any minute. He called me before he left the office," she said. She looked around the room as though it might be tapped.

"Mom, I'm in trouble."

"Baby, tell me what it is before your father—"

But it was too late. Through the door came Sister Louvois, followed by my father. The crease between his eyes was deeper, sharper.

"Will someone please tell me what this is all about?"

He was eyeing both of us, my mother and me, with Sister Louvois standing behind him with what I swore was a sneer on her face.

"Mr. Muchmore, I will gladly tell you the reason for this interruption," she said, gliding behind her desk. "Please, won't you take a seat next to your wife."

He looked at my mother as if she were a stranger and sat down. Out of the corner of my eye I saw her body shift slightly in my direction.

"Mr. and Mrs. Muchmore," Sister Louvois said, spreading her long, boney fingers on her desk. "I'm afraid that I—that *we*— have let you down."

My father shook his head. "I'm sorry, but I don't understand."

"Mr. Muchmore, we pride ourselves here at Saint Agnes for grooming our students to be in the likeness of the very saint for whom this school was named. We want our girls to leave here prepared to face the temptations of the world with grace and humility, and to understand the difference between what's right and what's wrong."

Pausing, Sister Louvois angled her eyes toward me. "With Lauren, however, we've already failed in that effort, and for that I am deeply remorseful."

Out of the top drawer of her desk she pulled out the manila envelope and passed its contents to my father. I watched him as he examined the letters, carefully turning the pages. Then with a shaking hand, he passed them one by one to my mother and began rubbing his forehead feverishly.

"I-I-I don't understand, Sister. These notes appear to be from someone named Daniel. Are you saying that Lauren's been indecent with a boy?"

"Not a boy, Mr. Muchmore. A man. The letters are from Daniel Krum."

It took my parents a moment or two to process this information. Then I thought my father's face was going to break.

"What? What are you talking about?" My father shot me a look that would have sliced through me if it had been a knife. "In God's name, that's . . . that's her *coach*!"

"Yes, I know, Mr. Muchmore. This news is quite disturbing to me as well."

"How did you get these?" my mother said. She leaned forward. "Are you sure they're not fakes?"

"Mrs. Muchmore," Sister Louvois said, turning to my mother. "They were left for me anonymously. And the reason I know they are genuine is because your daughter did not deny their authenticity."

"Have you talked to Daniel?" my father said with a hint of desperation in his voice. "Maybe she's just making this up?"

"To ensure the least amount of disruption to the students, I have not questioned him yet, no. But I intend to once classes are over at the end of the day."

"End of the day!" my father exploded. "That's not soon enough!"

"Mr. Muchmore, I promise you that Mr. Krum will undergo a complete investigation based on my conversation with Lauren today."

"And what did she say?"

"I suggest, sir, you ask your daughter yourself."

My father glanced a couple times in my direction before he addressed me. The way his lip curled and his eyes darted back and forth unnerved me.

"I-i-is it true, Lauren?" my father said, fumbling his words. "Did Coach Krum write these letters to you?"

"Yes," I said weakly, staring at my knees. "But Dad, it's—"

My father put up his hand. "Please don't say any more," he said, his voice softening. "You've said all that I need to hear."

After that, the room became still as death except for the faint sniffling of my mother into her tissue. And there had been a death, the death of my father's trust in me, the death of his hopes and dreams for me, the death of the good girl whom he could no longer claim as his own.

Sister Louvois watched from her mahogany desk as the news of my sin sunk in. I continued to pray, moving on to recite the Lord's Prayer silently to myself, more reverently than I ever had in my life.

"I'm sure you will agree that this cannot go unpunished," said Sister Louvois finally. "I'm going to recommend to Dr. Rainey that Lauren be suspended from classes and all school activities for the rest of the week."

"What about the state tournament?" my father spluttered.

"Mr. Muchmore, given that Lauren's participation on the basketball team was what led to this intolerable situation, I'm also going to recommend to Dr. Rainey that she be barred from the team for the rest of her time here at Saint Agnes."

My father sprang from his chair. "What?" he said. "But that was the whole reason she came to this school in the first place!"

"Mr. Muchmore." Sister Louvois's tone was tighter, sharper. "I'm sure you will agree that allowing your daughter to continue with her education here at Saint Agnes is more than generous. Prohibiting her from playing basketball is, in my opinion, letting her off easy, given the extent of the grievances against her."

"But what about him!" my mother said, standing up. "What about Daniel Krum? What will happen to him?"

"He will be dealt with appropriately, with the least amount of impact to the school and its students."

"That's not good enough," my mother said. "The authorities need to be called. We'll go to the papers!" It was the first time I'd ever heard her shout.

Sister Louvois stood and placed her hands on either side of her desk. Then she leaned in. "And risk putting undue attention on your family? Do you have any idea what they'd do with a story like this? I can see the headlines now," she said, waving her arm through the air. 'Fifteen-year-old girl has affair with high school coach.'"

My mother dropped back into her seat as if someone had cut her off at the knees. My father did the same.

Sister Louvois smoothed a strand of gray hair against her forehead. "I understand your frustration, really I do," she said, this time in a more tempered voice. "But it's my job to recommend what's best for Lauren and your family—that's my first priority. And I think drawing attention to the situation would cause more harm than good. Better to deal with it quietly behind closed doors."

She let my parents ponder this point for a moment and then continued on. "You must ask yourselves, would it really benefit your family to have police officers interrogating your daughter or reporters lined up on your front lawn?"

My mom shook her head.

"So let me do my job . . . let the school deal with this so no one, including your family, will get hurt."

My father finally broke his silence. "I don't know if I'm comfortable with this," he said. "Putting this all in your hands to fix."

"What *would* make you comfortable, Mr. Muchmore?" said Sister Louvois. Her voice was stern.

"Are we negotiating?"

"Carl, what are you doing?"

"Louise, stay out of this!"

"You can call it what you want, Mr. Muchmore."

"Then I want her to finish out the state tournament and I want him gone by the end of it."

"I can't do that—I can't let Lauren play any more basketball."

"Then this conversation is over and you'll be hearing from our attorney," said my father, rising from his chair.

"Wait!" said Sister Louvois, moving out from behind her desk. "Perhaps I'm being a bit rigid in my thinking. This would satisfy you, having Lauren play in the remaining state games?"

"At least that, yes, and removing *him* from your staff by the end of them."

Sister Louvois folded her arms against her chest. "I want you to know I'm not comfortable with this, Mr. Muchmore," she said. "But I'll allow it, just so we can peacefully put this behind us. Bear in mind though, aside from the state tournament, Lauren is to go nowhere near that court again."

Chapter 36

After that day in Sister Louvois's office, my parents never again spoke of my affair with Daniel Krum or even acknowledged its existence. Not once did they ask me how I came to be involved with a man more than twice my age. Nor did they demand to know what had gone on with him behind closed doors. They never screamed at me, became enraged or slapped me. Instead they did something that I considered much worse. They ignored me.

My mom was still talking to me at least, even if it was about mundane, everyday things. But my father? I might have well been invisible. He wouldn't look at me or even linger more than a minute in my presence. This was probably the hardest to take, the way he erased me. I wasn't used to my father not yelling and screaming at us, for that's how he did things—that's just how he was. But now the man who sat across from me at the dinner table barely able to bring his fork to his mouth and chew his food, the man who was looking more deflated and broken by the day, was suddenly a stranger to me, and not even the blood we shared was strong enough to forge a connection.

I sensed that my mother and sister were also waiting for him to explode. They too seemed to be stepping lightly through the house, as though fearing that if they made just one small misstep, they'd send my father into a fit of rage beyond anything we'd ever witnessed before. Even Carla was being cautious not to set him off. Although as my sister so readily pointed out, I'd most likely be the primary target of his wrath if he were to come unglued.

Yes, that's right. I actually had confided in Carla and told her everything that had happened with Daniel Krum. Well, almost everything. At the time I just couldn't bring myself to tell her about the pregnancy and what I had done about it. Trust me, I wanted to, but it wasn't until a few years later, when the painful memories had faded into shadows, that I finally had the strength to tell her. But when I did, she wrapped me in her arms and then gently asked me why it had taken me so long.

But getting to that point in our relationship took some time. Surprisingly, the whole thing with Daniel had a hand in bringing us closer, I think. Because let's face it, back when we were teenagers Carla was no angel, and hearing all the juicy details of my affair definitely whetted her appetite. Suddenly I became the little sister she had always wanted. I was following in her footsteps. I was living life on the edge. And maybe most importantly, just like her, I was a darkened star, tarnished by the wiles of love and the ruse of a man.

But even Carla hadn't done anything as shocking as having an affair with a married man. In her eyes, what I'd done was an awe-inspiring feat, especially the way I had managed to keep it all secret for so long and still maintain my role as the good little girl.

"Maybe that's what enticed him about you," she said dreamily as we lay on her bed, staring at the ceiling. "Maybe it was the whole schoolgirl thing that he couldn't resist."

"Maybe," I said reluctantly, hoping that my attractiveness to Daniel had gone deeper than just that of a teenage girl in a plaid skirt. But if that was really the reason, then why me? "There are countless girls at Saint Agnes who look like movie stars compared to me," I said. "I'm just so ordinary-looking, so awkward."

"I don't think so," said my sister, turning to me. "I've always wished that I was as tall and thin as you. And your skin— it reminds me of porcelain. It's so pretty."

"Then why do you always call me 'Güera'?"

She rolled on her back and tossed a decorative pillow into the air. "To get a rise out of you, why else?" I shrugged and a rolling laugh escaped Carla's painted red lips. "I just say it because I know it makes you squirm. But if it bothers you, I won't say it anymore."

I shrugged again. "It's not that it really bothers me all that much, it's just that you always say it so . . . *mean.*"

"Well, what if I don't say it like that anymore?"

I nodded and we were silent for a few minutes.

"Hey, Carla."

"Yeah."

"If it's any consolation, I've always wished that I had your boobs."

"Well you can have some of 'em, because there's plenty to go around."

"And Carla."

"What?"

"I think he might have really loved me."

"I wouldn't doubt it."

Not surprisingly, Carla had a pretty good handle on things when it came to boys, which came in handy when I knew I'd have to be in the same room as Daniel. She advised me to be all business around him and treat him like any other person on the street.

"Anything outside of basketball, just completely ignore him," she said.

Avoiding him turned out to be easier than I had thought, given that Sister Louvois had taken it upon herself to personally chaperone the team down to Houston for the state tournament, keeping her eyes on Daniel and me every step of the way. But our run for the state title was short-lived. We went home after a loss to a team from San Antonio in the second round, something I blamed myself for.

That weekend I played some of the worst basketball of my life, scoring not even close to my average of fourteen points a game. I just didn't have it in me anymore. The fire had gone out. And why try, anyway? Once the tournament ended, I'd most likely never pick up a basketball again.

Beth pretty much carried the team in the two games we played, but even her skillful dribbling and knack for dishing out passes wasn't enough. The chemistry the team once had enjoyed was pretty much a memory now, as was the charismatic man whom I had so eagerly at one time called my coach.

●●●

I think Daniel knew going into the tournament that it would mark his last days at Saint Agnes. But I don't believe he ever expected to leave the school in the way he did. Although I didn't get to see it firsthand, I heard that he was led away in the middle of his chemistry class. Some of the juniors in the room said that he didn't put up a fight, even as the officers turned him around to face the blackboard and cuffed his wrists behind his back. Word got around that as they led him out, he kept shaking his head and smiling, repeating under his breath that he'd done nothing wrong. And part of me wondered if he indeed had, and whether I should have been walked out right along with him.

I thought about him a lot in those days that followed. Had things at home become as bad for him as they had for me? I wondered how his wife was reacting and if they'd even stay married. I even wondered if little Skylar Krum ever would be allowed to touch the piano again.

Soon after Daniel's arrest, I learned that it was my mother who had tipped off the police. In hindsight she absolutely did the right thing, even though it caused the school, and everyone involved, a great deal of ridicule. But for someone whom I had always thought of as weak, my mother turned out to be quite the opposite. Perhaps it was all those years of getting beat up by my dad that had toughened her; or maybe it was really my mother who had for so long held together the jagged pieces of our family. Whatever the reason, her going public with the relationship also exposed the missteps of Sister Louvois, whom the school eventually removed from the post of vice principal.

But it also exposed my role in the whole scandal as well. Walking down those halls of Saint Agnes became a virtual nightmare, particularly on that day when I came upon a cluster of noisy upperclassmen gathered at my locker. Their giggling ceased as I edged closer, and like the Red Sea, they parted as I slowly walked through them. That's when I saw it—the word "WHORE" scribbled in big black letters across the front of my locker. And just like the judgmental eyes that Felicity faced at Pope Pius, I too suffered the scorn of my peers, diminishing what

I thought was my one and only love story into a laughable, dirty tale.

But even this wasn't as hurtful as my father's cold shoulder. I was shocked when he ended up making the trip to Houston to watch my last two games. While he still hadn't spoken to me since that day in Sister Louvois's office, it gave me a glimmer of hope seeing him in the bleachers, and I wondered if perhaps he was coming around. But just like he had done at home, he turned a blind eye to me at the tournament too, as if he were there to watch a daughter who didn't exist.

And so this silence of his continued, until late one night when he finally lost control.

I remember waking to what sounded like an animal in pain—a wailing so ghastly that for a minute I thought that whatever the thing was, it was dying right outside my window. Trembling in fear, I pulled on a sweatshirt and crept into the hall, looking up and down for any sign of the disturbance. Quietly I opened the door to Carla's room and peered in. Her bed was empty and the sheets disheveled.

The gruesome sound drew me into the kitchen and then out to the porch, where it led me across the lawn and over to the garage. Standing outside of it, I could hear the wailing clearly now, and the more tightly I pressed my ear against the weathered wood, the more alarmed I became. It sounded like a woman crying, or possibly a child—which one, I wasn't sure.

An image flashed in my mind's eye: my mother lying on the floor with blood spilling from her head. Then I saw my sister, slumped over and lifeless. "Mom!" I screamed as I rattled the doorknob that refused to give entry. "Carla!" But the wailing continued, echoing through the night. I rose up on my tiptoes and nervously pawed the rim of the door until I felt a key. I shoved it into the rusty lock, twisting and turning it and praying that I wasn't too late.

Then came a sudden shift in my point of view, a rearranging of my consciousness that I still struggle to understand. I was plucked out of my body and made a bystander, a duplicate as if by copy. I stood there observing myself—the entire scene—from a few yards away. I watched myself jimmy the lock, the image of a girl in pajama bottoms, a sweatshirt and socks, a girl so broken, so full of fear.

The lock gave way and I followed the trembling girl closely behind, one step at a time into a thin veil of darkness. She stopped abruptly and I reared up just in time before I smashed into the back of her head. We stood quietly for a moment, listening. Finally I stepped out from behind her and caught the image that had frozen her feet, my feet—our feet—so securely to the ground.

On the filthy floor of the garage, a shadow of my father lay curled in on himself, weeping uncontrollably. Each sob expanded in him a monstrous wave of despair. He didn't seem to know that we were there, or else he didn't let on.

I saw the other Lauren take a step forward, arms outstretched and body slightly bent. I saw her move toward her father, toward the man huddled on the ground, and extend her hand. But I lunged forward and grabbed her wrist, my wrist, and pulled back. Hard. Her head whipped around and she eyed me with a look of pure hatred, parting her lips just enough to expose the starkness of her teeth.

"No," I said. "You don't have to do this."

A mirror image of my face locked on mine. "Why? He needs my help."

I shook my head harder than I ever had before. She was right, but she was wrong. "No," I told her again. "This is not yours to carry. Not anymore."

The crease between her eyes softened as her mouth fell open.

I pulled her closer, wrapping my arms around her. "It's time that we protected each other. It's time to take care of ourselves."

When I felt the gentle pressure of her arms close around me, we shifted back into one body and mind. With my father's sobs crashing on the shore of my heart, I turned and walked back out into the cool air, closing the door softly behind me and then stretching up once more to place the key on the ledge.

Chapter 37

The next morning, my father left our house, taking with him all the pain and misery that had marked his presence. My mother really didn't go into detail as to where he'd gone, only saying that he had found a place of his own for the time being. She didn't speak of divorce or even separation. He was taking a break for a while, she said; for how long, she did not know.

As she spoke to us about him, I saw the confidence in her return, a confidence that I always thought had burned out long before I was born. It was the first time I'd ever seen her sprawled out in her own home, on her own sofa, shoulders relaxed and arms spread freely on the cushions, inhaling an atmosphere that no longer poisoned her spirit.

A couple days after my father left, my mom appeared in my doorway. With her arms gently crossed over her small frame, she leaned against the molding, waiting for me to invite her in.

"Hey, Mom."

A full smile spread across her face as she half danced into the room and lowered herself next to me on the bed. "Hey, baby. Whatcha doing?" I felt her petite hand stroke the side of my hair, twirl it up through her fingers and move it gently off my shoulder.

"Oh nothing," I said, closing my geometry book. "June's about to pick me up." I raised the thick textbook in the air. Need math help. Again."

My mother smirked and rolled her eyes. "Gosh, you're just like me. I thought math was some kind of alien language in high school."

I felt my breath hitch when I heard her speak those words. I wanted to submerge myself in them . . . capture them in a jar so I could prove that they were real. *Just like me.* Like my mom. Me, a part of her. Us, one like the other.

I felt her cool fingertips touch the top of my hand and then curl around my palm. I looked into eyes that I knew to be mine, although years older and much too tired.

"Baby, I wanted to tell you something." My mother spoke in a gentle, soothing tone. "I want you to know that"—she paused, drawing a breath—"that if you ever need to talk about anything, I'm here, okay?"

I let go of her eyes and dropped mine to the floor. "Hmm-mm," I mumbled, gripping the shag carpet with my toes.

She released my hand and placed her cool fingers on either side of my face. "Lauren, look at me, honey." Slowly I raised my eyes to hers, locking on them tighter than before. Her lips parted and moved, but I couldn't make out a thing she was saying. It's like my ears had turned off or were revolting against the words. She frowned, sharpening the creases on her face. Moving closer into my eyes, she moved her lips again. And this time I heard every single word.

"Lauren, none of it was your fault."

My heart raced and I shook my head. "What wasn't my fault?"

Her eyes smiled wide, spilling tears down her cheeks. "Everything and nothing, baby. Everything and nothing."

• • •

My mother's words stuck with me as I climbed in June's Bronco that afternoon, trying desperately to act like everything was normal, like I was normal as she blasted the stereo. I drummed my thighs trying to play along, but all I could think of as the wind whipped through my hair from the open window was my piece in all of this, in all that had gone so wrong. Yet for a moment, for only a fleeting moment and nothing more, I actually felt the heavy weight of guilt lift from my shoulders, only to have it force me down again when my thoughts shifted to the life I had erased.

Even now, even twenty-five years later, there's still not a day that goes by that I don't think of that child and what could have been—the color of her eyes, the texture of her hair, the sound of her voice. She still visits me in my sleep, sometimes older, sometimes younger, but always gazing at me with those deep blue eyes. Her face is soft and relaxed, never tight or strained. And then, oh yes, this is what I love most, she smiles at me, and I feel like the luckiest woman in the world, lucky to have her visit me one more time and forgive me once more.

If I'm ever going to recover and move forward with my life, I will have to lay down my guilt and let the tide take it away. Therapy is helping . . . a little, I guess. But some days I still feel deep in the hole, with no glint of light to guide my way out. That's when my memory of him, of us together, rises to life, and every emotion that ever ached in me comes flooding back. The desire. The guilt. The longing. The unbearable weight of sin. And suddenly, I'm little fifteen again, spellbound by the one Daniel Krum; stumbling over myself in my mad schoolgirl crush; blushing my way back into my blissful schoolgirl dream.

Acknowledgments

The second generation of this novel was born from my accidental friendship with best-selling author E.L. Farris. E.L. saw the healing power of Lauren's story and didn't let up until I agreed to take back ownership and make it the book it was meant to be.

From there, God revealed to me a team of individuals that was instrumental in taking Lauren's story to the next level. I'm grateful to my editor, Christina M. Frey, for challenging me to stretch my skills as a writer, and for helping me make *Little 15* better than it started; my cover designer, Brent Meske, for his endless creativity and enthusiasm; author Bobbie L. Parish, for her friendship, and the hours and energy she put into proofing this book; to my friends and family for their encouragement and support; and to the hundreds of fans and readers who connect with my characters and keep coming back for more.

My art would be nothing without the backbone that is my family—my husband, Rick, and my sons, Ian and Luke—who so often share me with the imaginary people in my head. I love you to the moon and back, and then back around again.

And finally, thank you to my favorite band, Depeche Mode, whose song *Little 15* inspired the title for this novel. There are emotions and situations in this book that were influenced by the brilliance and beauty of Depeche Mode songs. You forever have a fan in me.

Love and light.

Stephanie Saye

About the Author

Stephanie Saye

Like *Little 15's* Lauren Muchmore, Stephanie played varsity basketball for an all-girls Catholic high school—and she really did get policed by nuns on the way to class. Stephanie has since traded in her Nike high-tops for Brooks running shoes (and her corporate career for the life of a novelist and screenwriter). She lives in Texas with her husband and two sons.

Stephanie is also the author of the screenplay adaptation of *Little 15*, and the upcoming novel *Sawtooth*.

Stephanie loves to talk with readers (and she answers all of her correspondence personally!). Connect with her on:
- Facebook (http://facebook.com/StephanieSaye)
- Twitter (@StephanieSaye)
- Goodreads
- email (authorstephaniesaye@gmail.com).

If you would like to be notified when Stephanie's next book is released and about other related news, please visit her author website, http://stephaniesaye.com, to subscribe to e-mail updates.

Little 15: The Movie

Film producers have already expressed interest in making this story into a movie for general theatrical release, and will pursue that after a sufficient number of books are in circulation. Word of mouth is still the most effective tool for a book like this to gain wider distribution and exposure.

If you've been touched by Lauren's story, and want to help make it available to others on a broader level, please help spread the word by:

- Leaving a brief review on Amazon (http://tinyurl.com/little15saye).
- Sharing the book on your Facebook page, Twitter feed, and/or blog.
- Asking your favorite radio show or podcast to have the author on as a guest.
- Suggesting it for book clubs in your area.

For more up-to-date information, please visit:

www.stephaniesaye.com

www.ingramcontent.com/pod-product-compliance
Lightning Source LLC
Chambersburg PA
CBHW051250250626
47155CB00009B/3247